LIOPLEURODON

IAN WOODHEAD

SEVERED PRESS

HOBART TASMANIA

LIOPLEURODON

PROLOGUE

They rose from the cold ocean depths together, both eager to fill their stomachs with soft, warm meat. It had been many weeks since either of them fed on anything larger than the ever present young of their old enemy. If they did not find something substantial soon, their unborn calf would not survive birth, meaning their kind would die too. He knew that the scent of death leaving her body would send him into a feeding frenzy, and she would retaliate and try to kill him. Although the calf may be dead, her maternal instinct would take longer to dissipate.

If it hadn't been for the seaquake, their kind would already have perished. The rocks which had confined their kind and their food for untold millennia crumbled when the very earth threatened to consume them.

Their food had long gone from their kingdom. Only the small animals remained, and they were difficult to catch. Not that it mattered now. This sea teemed with unlimited amounts of food. The quantity almost overpowered his senses. He would soon be feasting again.

The female released a single call before turning around and swimming in the opposite direction. She had warned him not to follow, for she was soon ready to give birth and did not want the huge bull to threaten her young.

He allowed her to go, knowing that she would be ready for him once her calf was ready to leave her. All that mattered now was the pursuit of his prey.

CHAPTER ONE

Old Meg Grey wasn't going to let her two unwanted visitors steal her food without a fight. It had taken her ages to open that parcel jammed full of rotting fish pieces. Mr Scar and his new friend might be twice her size, but their bulk didn't amount for shit when Old Meg Grey flew at them, screaming like a banshee, her long claws tearing into their bodies while she did her best to peck out their eyes.

That seagull was one mean hombre. None of the other birds, even the two gulls larger than her, couldn't get anywhere near those kitchen scraps when she was around. The bird pushed her beak inside the hole she'd cut into the plastic and gulped down most of the contents while keeping a watchful eye on the other approaching scavengers.

Mr Scar then developed a streak of courage which Maddock Tailor had never noticed before. The younger gull hopped towards Meg Grey. He grabbed the plastic bag and pulled it backwards. As soon as her head was clear, the gull spread his wings, threw his body off the thick wall, and dived towards the Atlantic. The older bird then made the biggest mistake of her life by chasing after Mr Scar while screeching her rage.

Maddock tightened his grip on the scaffold rail surrounding the compound. If the guards saw him leaning over the edge, they'd take away his privileges. Right at that moment, they could even throw him in the hole as long as they allowed him to watch how the drama on the kitchen roof concluded.

The younger seagull had already flown all the way around the prison facility before Meg Grey had time to realise that she'd never catch him. He screeched in triumph as he flew away. The older bird returned to what was once her domain, only to find that the compressed mass of grey and white feathered noisy carpet did not want her to land. Oh, she clawed and frantically flapped her wings, but none of them yielded.

The incredible noise from their fury blotted out everything else.

Maddock sensed the conversations from the others behind him had ceased in response to the unexpected break in their monotonous routine. Only he knew full well that the seabirds having a bit of a barney wasn't the real reason as to the abrupt change. His instincts were already more active than usual; they had been over-active ever since the head screw announced yard time once the clouds had finally broken.

Right now, Maddock's every sense tingled. If they were going to do it, this was the ideal time. The birds continued their noisy riot, still refusing to let the older bird access to the few paltry scraps available. He leaned a little more over the edge just to give whoever was to take up the challenge, their optimum chance.

Sure enough, a brief shadow passed across his left eye. He feinted to the side then dropped to the concrete and rolled back, missing the unknown attacker's shank sticking into his inner thigh by seconds. Maddock rolled on his back and snapped both legs out, grunting in satisfaction as his boots smacked into the top of the man's ankles.

His face smacked into the metal railing. Even with the furious bird cries, Maddock was sure he heard the sound of bone cracking. Maddock jumped up. He booted the man between the legs. He didn't have long left. The sirens had already begun to wail. Maddock needed to finish this right now!

He spun the man around, not altogether surprised to find himself staring into the bloodied face of little soapy Johnson. Again, he wasn't surprised. Not many in here would be stupid enough to try to end him despite the sizeable reward offered. Then again, everybody knew that thanks to his obsessive gambling problem, it was only a matter of time before The Beast in Cell nine offered Soapy's life out for collection.

His fastened his fingers around the old man's scrawny neck, now fully aware of steel studded boots slamming into the compound floor. He had about ten seconds left. "Heads or tails, Soapy?"

"What?"

"Answer or die."

The man's eyes darted left then to the right before settling on the guards who were almost on top of them.

"Heads," he replied.

He obviously thought he was safe now which probably explained the smug grin. "Wrong answer," snarled Maddock before squatting down and grabbing Soapy's ankles. Maddock stood up bringing the ankles with him. Two guards reached the man just as he tossed Soapy over the railing. Their electro sticks slammed into his side, thighs and arms, sending his body into a spasm of convulsive shock. Whatever probable thoughts of attacking the screws went right out the window when they hit him with the voltage. Not that he had any. He guessed they didn't know that. After all, Maddock had just thrown another prisoner over the railing.

The sticks left him as weak as a newborn baby. He was also vaguely aware that he had fouled himself. Not that he could do anything about it. The screws had chained his arms together and were currently smashing their black-gloved fists into every part of his upper body. None of them marked his face; they weren't that stupid.

The sirens abruptly stopped at the same time as two senior guards, the deputy warden, and three white coated doctors from the prison hospital raced across the yard. Maddock tried to tell the doctors that they'd need plastic bags and a shovel for that clown, but all he managed to do was to drool out long strings of thick saliva.

The guard got him onto his feet while the deputy warden continued the job that his subordinates had started but this time on his face. Maddock didn't mind. The electro sticks had already fried his pain impulses. It would be a good few hours before they started working again. By that time, he'd be in a bed, doped up on painkillers.

In between the deputy warden's punches, Maddock saw the rest of the prisoners stood on the metal benches at the back of the compound shouting and jeering. He noticed the only two friends he had in this hell-hole doing exactly the same as the others. Not that he blamed them. The rest of those freaks would have kicked the crap out of the pair of them.

He wished he knew the betting. Maddock would have put half a pack of snout on the deputy warden busting his cheek bones before he hit the deck. The siren blared out again just before Maddock's brain was about to throw in the towel. The Deputy warden immediately put his hands down. He then snatched a silver flask from the waiting hand of a screw. He took off the cap, had a swift swig, and spat the contents of his mouth into Maddock's face.

"We can't have you passing out on us, 15352. No way, not when we have so much more planned for you. I need to continue this cosy chat somewhere without an audience." The deputy warden snapped his fingers; two screws grabbed an arm each and marched him past the other prisoners. His two friends were still putting up a great performance, but Maddock saw the pain in their eyes. He saw hate in the eyes of the other prisoners as well as respect. He might be the freak's main target, but Maddock was still one of them.

This would be another bad session, but Maddock would endure, just he had endured the other beatings they'd given him since he arrived at Stone Yield penitentiary, an impregnable fortress which is totally escape proof. There was no way out unless any potential escapee wanted to swim home.

They had built Stone Yield in the middle of the Atlantic Ocean on an artificial island a thousand miles from the nearest land. Maddock did intend to escape, to try to find some way off this rock, to return home, and to somehow clear his name.

The jeering had lessened by the time they had reached the first compound exit gate. The fun was over. Maddock hadn't fallen which, no doubt, earned a couple of inmates an extra bar of soap or a few more smokes. The two screws at his side made him stop while their boss pressed in a five-digit code before pressing his forefinger against the glass window in the door panel. A blue light blinked twice before the first door opened. Maddock listened to the door close and seal while wondering if he'd ever see daylight again. It's doubtful that the warden would allow him to continue to be a trustee once he got wind of this. If, that is, Maddock lived through the next beating.

The psycho in front of him, now opening the door which led into the prison's upper level, wasn't exactly gentle with the tools he kept in his private office. In fact, the beatings were getting progressively longer. Maddock didn't know if that was part of the program or if the deputy warden's sadistic affliction was getting worse.

Suffice to say that if these beatings did continue there wouldn't be much left of him to escape. Damien Allen, otherwise known as Blakey, his current cellmate, had already warned him to keep his head down and to stay out of everybody's way. Easier said than done when trouble actively sought him out.

His other friend, Stix the fixer, had offered him similar advice, only he told him in no uncertain terms that the freak wanted him dead, and the only way to appease him would be to show that Maddock was as ruthless as him.

The two guards pushed him forward. Maddock managed to stay on his feet as they shoved him into the upper level. Stix had also warned him that Soapy would look for an opportunity today and not for the first time, Maddock silently questioned his friend's loyalty. Could he, too, be part of the conspiracy to keep his awareness levels on full throttle? It was getting to the point where loyalty and betrayal were merging into one. Both Stix and that sad excuse of the human could be working for the government; it's not like he could find out whilst trapped in here.

Until seven months ago, Maddock worked for an obscure branch of the government who were tasked with diplomatic safety and security to making sure their overseas special visitors never came to any harm.

His team had overseen the safety of hundreds of foreign dignitaries, keeping them safe from threats both from their own countries and from any potential threat from their land and from overseas. Until seven months ago, their reputation was spotless, their team was beyond exemplary. At least until they were tasked in protecting a North Korean party assigned to them. The plans were proceeding on schedule until three armoured cars pulled up beside their own armoured car and opened fire. He was the only one to live through the assault. Upon arrival of the company's security team, they had arrested and charged Maddock of their murder and of larceny. The company had already seized his bank accounts and apparently found over two million dollars inside.

As far as the government was concerned, he was a danger to himself and the country, hence the reason why they dropped him in here. Maddock had often wondered why they hadn't just killed him after the trial and the trumped-up charges. Damien had told him the only reason he could think of as to why Maddock still lived was so they could bring out their scapegoat again, perhaps at a time when his presence could mean the difference between tyranny and annihilation. Damien refused to expand on his cryptic answer apart from to remind him that North Korea did have nuclear weapons.

"Prisoner 12329s body smashed against the rocks."

The deputy warden leaned closer. Under the almost overpowering smell of mint toothpaste, Maddock detected salsa as well as brandy. He smiled back. "Not even all the king's horses and all the king's men will be able to put him back together."

"I was going to try to appeal to your human side, but it's now clear to me that you don't have one. Of course, you don't; you're just an animal, a rabid dog."

Was it worth telling this overweight, balding, middle-aged prick what the cook's trustee did to the salsa? Probably not; this idiot wouldn't believe him anyway.

"Officer Jones, what do we do with rabid dogs?"

"We put them down, sir."

"Then why is he still breathing? Jones, hand me your weapon."

The officer dutifully did as he was ordered. Like the deputy warden and the other guard, Officer Jones was enjoying himself immensely. Maddock felt the cold metal against his forehead, and for a moment, imagined his spirit looking down at his shattered corpse while the three men ran around in circles like headless chickens, all trying to think of some explanation that could cover their stupid mistake. Not that they would kill him in here. Where was the fun in that? Dead people didn't feel pain.

"Sir!" hissed Jones, he's left his office."

"Shit." the deputy warden pulled the prisoner over the nearest door and swiped his card through the lock. "Get him in here; I'll see if I can push the old man back into his office. Dammit, what's he doing out so early?"

So that was his game! The warden obviously didn't have a clue at what his second in command and his two stooges were getting up to behind his back. There was no conspiracy; the man just enjoyed hurting people, and Maddock was unlucky enough to be his latest target.

They pulled him into the room. Jones shut the door, plunging them into pitch black.

"The light, Jones," hissed his colleague. "We're not moles."

Harsh white light flooded the confined room. Brown cardboard boxes surrounded the three men on two sides. Jones pressed his ear against the door.

"They're both outside now."

If he wasn't so weak, Maddock would have screamed out or lunged forward and slammed the side of the screw's head into that wooden panel. It turned out that he wasn't the only one to think of that possibility. The other screw placed his sweaty hand over Maddock's mouth while his other arm wrapped around the prisoner's waist. "Keep very still, 15352,"

Maddock jerked backwards. He blinked rapidly. What was that? Had he just had a dizzy spell, or did the ground suddenly move? He turned his head to find Jones staring up towards the ceiling. Maddock followed his line of sight and watched a single apple roll along the top of the boxes before it fell off the edge and hit the metal deck close to Jones's boots.

"What's going on?" he whispered. "Is it an earthquake?"

The vibrations grew more violent. Maddock found himself free as the other officer stumbled over to the door. Both of them struggled to get the door open while the room continued to shake. He dropped to his knees and leaned against the boxes. In his weakened state, it was the best he could manage.

A couple of boxes fell from the top and landed behind him just before he and the two men found themselves thrown backwards. They all landed together in a pile of arms and legs while the shaking room refused to slow down. Boxes rained down on them.

Maddock heard the other two shouting and cursing while trying to crawl out from under the boxes. He stayed put, knowing what little strength he had would all but give out if he attempted to follow the. Even if he did, then what? Maddock severely doubted that the shaking was confined to this room.

To prove his point, the door burst open inwards, spilling cold sea water into the room. Both officers got to their feet and stumbled through the open door. Neither of them looked back to see if he was following.

He curled his fingers around the wet cardboard and groaned softly as the whole room tilted. Somewhere close by, a man cried out, and his voice carried the sound of pain as well as terror. Then the room tilted again. More boxes fell onto his body, and then that voice cut off in mid scream.

His instincts, as weak as they were, told him that the water had brought something else into this prison. That if he wanted to stay alive, Maddock needed to stay quiet and not to move. Another man's shrieking blasted into his room, closely followed by one more. Maddock had to press his hands against his ears when it sounded like every prisoner on the rock was now screaming, yet even the cacophony of human voices could not compete with a new noise which shook the room and turned the marrow in Maddock's bones to liquid.

Even with his hands pressed tight against his ear, Maddock could not blot out that deep, thunderous noise which overpowered everything else. He opened his mouth, knowing that his own scream was about ready to blast out.

Another box fell and landed on his back, knocking him to the floor, and forcing the air out of his lungs. Maddock lay shivering in the cold water still needing the scream when he saw the door move again. He raised his head slightly, getting ready to shout out when the stench of a million rotting fish took away his breath. Maddock lowered his body slowly behind the tumbled boxes when he caught sight of something grey and shiny move past the gap between the door and the wall.

For the first time since childhood, Maddock found himself utterly terrified; and he didn't know why.

CHAPTER TWO

Three hundred miles south

It amazed Georgia Sandhurst how that man could find fault in just about everything his pale blue eyes rested on. Two minutes ago, it was the odd taste of his coffee; of course, the loaded insinuation was aimed at her, that she was responsible for the altering the already foul taste of this liquid mud simply by passing it from the automatic dispenser next to her and over the vacant seat between them.

Captain Liam Holmes always insisted that the co-pilot's seat in Echo-Babylon's Nautilus class submersible remained empty unless, of course, Georgia could prove to him that she was fully qualified to sit in it. She wasn't born yesterday. The only reason why he wanted that seat empty was because the man simply hated anybody near him, and the thought of another person brushing against his body while he operated the machine would drive the man insane.

Such a shame really, considering the view from there was utterly mesmerising. A thick cross beam slit her view into three. She listened to the man mutter under his breath for a couple of seconds before turning away. Georgia didn't want the man having another go at her. Not for the first time she wondered if he ever smiled. She found herself doing the exact thing at the thought of how many hearts back at the resort this gruff, thick set man would melt if he did turn that frown of his upside down.

Georgia would love to give Liam a complete make over to see exactly what lay under that oily overall that he never takes off. Probably more oil. Still, under that there would be something hunky enough to sink her teeth in - once she'd scrubbed him down first, obviously.

"Are you paying attention to the instruments?"

"Of course, I am," she replied, miffed at herself for not noticing Liam glaring at her. "No change. Whatever anomaly they saw back at the base has long gone. I still think it was some passing whale."

"Just keep watching that screen, Georgia. If there is something of that mass close by, it could create considerable damage to our attractions. Can't be caught with our pants down." He turned away and busied himself in focussing on his own display panel.

"I can't imagine you being caught with your pants down, Liam. Mainly because you never take off that overall. In fact, there's a rumour going around that you've Velcroed your pant seam for quick access when you visit the toilet."

"Eyes to screen, please," he said, without turning around.

"Yes, my master," she replied before ignoring him and pressing her nose against the thick Plexiglass curved screen instead. Georgia watched a large school of tiny fish swim through the skeletal remains of their wrecked 17th century Spanish galleon. She found it absolutely fascinating how the local wildlife adapted to the human's encroachment into their territory with ease. Even the fish dancing through the ship matched the colour of the coral covering the galleon's timber.

"Can you see anything?"

"Yep, there's a thousand tiny yellow fish, some wonderful looking coral, and a great big, stupid fake ship."

"That twenty-seven million dollar installation, along with the several other attractions that are tethered to the outer base, is what's keeping you in your job."

"You don't really believe that rubbish. They came to Echo-Babylon for the prestige; to show off and to brag that they were rich enough to holiday in the world's most expensive resort. I suspect they also come here for the drugs and women."

"You have a very cynical attitude towards our guests."

"Come on, Liam. Do you honestly think that Sir Moneybags Smythe from England is going to be wondering why there's an old-fashioned shipwreck which seems to be floating six thousand metres above the ocean floor while snorting self-raising flour?" She sighed. "Oh, and let's not forget some high-class tart on his bed covering her thighs in fresh cream."

"Yes well, what the guests do in privacy is their own business. Now, enough of this. I need you to keep your attention on the scope, Georgia. If something big does hit those wires, the damage caused could be severe enough to close the resort."

Reluctantly, she sat back in her white leather chair and paid attention to her scope. Georgia had no wish to use up the man's daily word number before the end of her shift. "Sorry, boss. The scope is clear. There's nothing out there larger than us."

"Good. We'll give it a few more minutes before we head back. I'll move us towards the U-boat. There's fewer objects there to confuse the instruments."

Georgia watched the little machine glide past the pretend wreck while allowing her mind to wander. She would be twenty-eight next month. How sad was that? Here she was, almost in her thirties, still single, gradually losing her good looks, and watching her career flushing down the toilet. It came to something when the best her doctorate in marine archaeology could get her was floating about in a watertight bathtub with a man who smelled worse than a pensioned off camel, and with a personality to match.

She should be working in the Med, looking for Roman wrecks; it's where her two best friends from university ended up. One of her friends had even found herself diving off the coast of Australia and working with some of the best sonar equipment on the planet, while she had to make do with looking at made up wrecks. It's like life was playing some cruel joke on her.

He leaned forward and frowned at something outside. Had Liam ever been kissed? Georgia was seriously considering making this man her next project. It certainly would be a feather in her cap if she did manage to bed him. Georgia would be the envy of the resort's female staff, that's for sure. Those big hands were so dexterous. She had watched him fixing broken machinery in his workshop. She bet he could do all sorts of pleasurable things with those fingers.

"That is very strange," he muttered. "Has the scope altered in any way?"

Georgia jerked herself back to reality and found herself frowning as well. "Must be ghosting or something." She looked at him then turned her attention back to the cold ocean beyond the submersible. "The scope is telling me that there's two U-boats out there."

As soon as the word left her mouth, Liam immediately switched off the front spotlights and killed the motors, leaving machine vulnerable to the ocean currents.

"What did you do that for?"

"You're the one with the qualifications," he snapped, while dimming the lights in the cockpit. "Join the dots, lady."

She refused to let him goad her. Georgia bit back a retort and unbuckled her seat belt instead. She had a better idea.

"What the hell are you doing?"

His growing alarm was like music to her ears. Liam became even more agitated when she climbed into the seat next to him. "Thanks to you, there's hardly any light. I can't see all the way back there." She settled in the seat, more interested in watching him than whatever was going on out there. Liam was incredibly uncomfortable by her proximity but didn't say anything.

"Oh, my God," he murmured." I thought so. Look, Georgia. Look at that!"

She saw the whale at the same time he spoke. Georgia watched, spellbound, as the creature poked its head past the bow of the imitation U-boat. "I don't believe it. A North Atlantic Right Whale. Have you any idea how rare they are?"

He nodded. "I call her Daisy. This is the first time she's ventured so close to the resort though. Something must have spooked her."

The man sitting next to her felt like a completely different person. The tense muscles and nervous disposition had left Liam. Georgia could strip naked and paint herself blue, and he wouldn't notice. Then again, she couldn't blame him. The animal was magnificent. "You've seen her before?"

"A couple of times, but not this close." He wiped the glass. "I wonder where the other one's got to? He can't be far."

Liam's hand edged towards the control joystick until at the last minute when it looked like he'd

remembered the motors were off. He grinned. "Wait, there he is. There's little Harry. Not that he's all that little now."

He couldn't be older than a year. Georgia watched the baby whale dart out past his mother before quickly turning back and disappearing behind the U-boat. "It looks like they're playing hide and seek with us, but I doubt they are." She glanced at Liam. "How did they get through the nets?"

The contractors had erected steel-reinforced netting around and under the floating resort specifically to stop larger animals from entering and causing damage to the visual attractions, as well as to provide a shark free environment for the tourists who wished to explore these pretend sunken wrecks. Liam had taken her on Georgia's first venture in the resort's Nautilus craft to examine the protective netting a few weeks ago. The sheer scale of it astonished her. It ran for miles around the resort.

"You told me that no creature alive could get through that stuff."

"Yeah, I did," he replied, not taking his eye off the mother whale. "It's doubtful that they squeezed through the holes, and they can't break it, so we're looking for another reason. "My money is on human intruders. I guess we had better report this in. They'll need to know where the breach is as well."

"Wait, does this vessel have anything to protect us? You know, torpedoes or grenades or something?"

"Where do you think you are, lady? This isn't a Trident submarine. We have powerful lights and a fast engine."

She nodded. "You think they'll be able to help that baby whale? I've figured out what she's doing. There must be a school of sharks close by. She is protecting the baby."

"No, not a chance; the scope would have picked them up. I'm still going for human activity." He went towards the starter motor only to find her fingers wrapping around his wrist.

"Listen to me, Liam. Whales won't react like that near a few idiots in scuba suits. Trust me on this. After all, I'm the one with the qualifications, remember?"

"And I'm telling you there's nothing here apart from us and the whales. The scope doesn't lie." He tapped the side of his headset. "Control, this is EBN1. Sightings confirmed. There's a couple of whales within the protected zone. Yes, you heard me, Control. I did say bloody whales. No, of course we can't shoot them. Look, go get Tony. Are you being funny? Where else am I going to go?"

While Liam raged at Tony, she stared through the window, wishing she had brought her camera. Georgia also wished that he'd stopped the craft a little closer to the U-boat, as right now there were drifting back towards the galleon.

Several yellow fish darted past the side of the submersible. She gave them a little wave. The young woman then clapped excitedly when the baby whale pushed past her mum and swam towards the fish. It might only be a baby, but the animal was still twice the size of this craft, and she knew that if that whale just happened to hit them they could end up getting wet very quickly. Even a glancing blow from that tail could cause serious damage.

"They're bringing in some experts from the mainland. They also agree with you about no human interference. Tony just happened to mention that, instead of spending hours cutting through the net, all they had to do was jump over the top."

She laughed. "Told you. Next time listen to me. I'm the one with qualifications."

"Yeah well, I..." Liam's hands snapped forward and pulled her tight into his embrace. "Holy shit!" he yelled as the submersible violently rocked from side to side."

"What the hell is going on?"

Liam sat her back down and buckled Georgia into the seat. "Look at that!"

The view had turned yellow. She had never seen anything like it in her life. There were thousands of fish in front of them, all swimming in one huge school heading in the same direction as the other few fish.

Liam looked straight at her. "I think you were right; a shark must have followed the whales into the protected zone. "It'll be after the baby."

"What can we do?"

"Don't worry, Georgia. There's no shark alive that would dare attack baby, not with mum so close."

Liam tapped his headset, paused, then tapped it again. Instead, he reached for the instruments. "We better report this in person." He grinned. "The Nautilus is supposed to be shark proof, but I'm not taking any chances, not with you on board."

"Thank you. I think that's the sweetest thing you've ever said to me."

"Yeah, well, if you did end up dead, they'd have me cooped up in some damned office for hours filling in forms." He started up the little craft. "I can't stand paperwork."

He had a cruel sense of humour; this was getting better and better. Liam hadn't ordered her back to the other seat either. Georgia turned her head and stared at the black bulk next to them, wishing that the huge galleon was real. While she was in fantasy land, she also wished that Liam would embrace her again. That was nice.

"I'd better get us moving."

"Wait, hang on." She leaned forward. "I think there's something inside that galleon, Liam. I could swear I saw something moving."

"Maybe it's our mysterious visitor," he replied. "If there is a shark in there, that will explain why the fish left so quickly." Liam reached for the lights. "It will also explain why nothing appeared on the scope."

"It's too big to be a shark."

The two ultra bright spotlights flooded the Galleon's interior with harsh white light which cut through the gloom like a hot knife through butter. Georgia shrieked in utter shock as a creature longer than an articulated truck shot out of the interior, heading straight for them. "Kill the lights!" she screamed.

Liam slammed the control stick to the left lurching the craft away from the monster's cavernous mouth. "What the bloody hell is it? That's no shark."

Georgia gripped the sides of her seat, unable to take her eyes off it. The creature was the same length as that mother whale but sleeker and with four paddle like limbs. It was the sight of that nightmarish head full of dagger-sized teeth which threatened to turn her into a tight ball of quivering flesh.

Liam killed the lights and slid the Nautilus out of the monster's path. "You okay?"

Georgia managed to nod even though she was anything but okay. "We are in the shit now," she whispered, unable to take her eyes off the monster as it gracefully slid past their machine. "That's a Liopleurodon. A Jurassic predator." She wanted to close her eyes and pretend that this wasn't really happening, that she was watching some dumb simulation which the lecturers back at uni were so fond of.

"Wait, Liam. That thing out there is real. I mean, it isn't some animatronic attraction they didn't bother telling us about!"

He shook his head, then pushed the control stick forward. "No, it's real. As real as we are. It's been hunting the whales."

"Liam, come on. We need to go back. You have no idea what this means!"

He shook his head. "Oh, believe me, I do know."

"Then what the hell are you doing?" Georgia thought her head was going to explode.

"We need evidence." His fingers danced over his control screen. "Getting some footage. Otherwise, who is going to believe us? Unless you want me to radio in that there's a prehistoric sea monster swimming through the installations." He squeezed her hand. "Hey, calm down. Don't worry; it won't attack us."

Georgia sighed. She felt so numb. Did he not understand that this shouldn't be happening? That animal went extinct a hundred and fifty million years ago. How could the man be so bloody calm?

"It's likely to hunt by smell," he continued. "And the Nautilus certainly doesn't smell like prey. Besides, it has already chosen its next meal."

Even the warmth of his hand gave her no comfort. "Do you understand, Liam. This is impossible."

Liam leaned across, grabbed both side of her head, then gave her a deep sensual kiss. "Better?" he asked. Pulling away, he said, "Now listen to me, Georgia. We have only explored about five percent of our oceans. We don't have a clue what lives in the depths below us. Don't make me kiss you again," he said, smiling.

"But it shouldn't exist!" she protested.

"Yeah, I know, but the same goes for crocodiles and turtles. I learned a long time ago to never underestimate nature. Now come on, Georgia. I need you to be functional. I can't do this without you."

The mother whale swam in a tight circle, protecting her calf while the huge creature raced towards them. Although the same length as the mother whale, Georgia knew that the animal stood little chance of surviving the attack. Her only hope was for her to abandon her baby, but there was no way that would happen.

"Close your eyes, Georgia."

She couldn't do it. No matter how hard she tried, Georgia could not turn away as the Liopleurodon reached the mother whale. The monster opened its jaws and ripped out a large chunk of the whale's stomach. It then turned and bit her tail clean off. "Have you got enough footage? Please tell me you have. I think I'm going to be sick."

"Yeah, come on, let's get you back, Georgia." he paused. "Your monster has enough food there to stop it from following us back to the resort."

Blood and shredded flesh billowed from the severed body as the corpse began to sink. Georgia knew she was crying but didn't care. There was only Liam with her, and she suspected that he was feeling just as distraught. All that mess clouded up the water making it difficult to make out if the baby had managed to escape those huge jaws. Georgia couldn't see it anywhere.

"Close your eyes, Georgia."

She wanted to do as he suggested, but she couldn't look away. Georgia needed to see the baby swimming away. Surely that monster wouldn't go for the baby, not when it had so much food right there next to it. She jumped in her seat when the little craft bumped against something.

"Calm down, lady. We've just touched the galleon. Nothing to be scared of."

She caught a flash of yellow in the corner of her eye. The yellow fish were back. Georgia found herself calming down a little. The monster hadn't moved out of that cloud of guts, so she assumed that it was busy feeding on the corpse, meaning that the baby had probably gotten away.

Georgia focused on the pretty fish. There were about thirty of them grouped together close to the craft by Liam's side. "Let's go back, Liam. Please."

"Okay, but no lights. I don't want to draw that things attention."

He activated the motor and nudged the Nautilus away from the pretend wreckage and straight into the path of the yellow fish. The tiny animals scattered, revealing why they'd been grouped so tightly together. The fish were feasting on a piece of whale flesh. She leaned towards the screen and immediately wished she hadn't. The turbulence spun it around, revealing a tiny torn off fin.

Liam moved the craft away from the installation while keeping a worried gaze on his control screen. "Don't worry. We'll be back before you know it. I guess it was the dinosaur thing which hit through the netting."

"Liopleurodon," she replied, automatically.

"Whatever it's called. My point is that it'll be doubtful that the monster will be leaving any time soon, meaning that the authorities will be able to deal with it easy enough."

"If they believe the footage. I saw it with my own eyes, and I'm having difficulty coming to terms with it."

"Don't worry about that," he replied, smiling. "I have an idea what to do." Liam tapped his headset. "Control, we have identified the course of the breach. There's a killer whale loose in the zone. Yes. You heard me right, a killer whale. You need to get in touch with the authorities. As soon as possible. This thing is huge. The biggest I've ever seen." He winked at Georgia. "Yes, I've turned out the lights so I don't draw its attention." Liam tapped his headset. "Okay, that's done. I think I need a drink."

Georgia took hold of his hand. "So do I." She squeezed tight. "And you can pay." Georgia blinked rapidly when their destination suddenly lit up.

"They've just activated every floodlight on the resort! The idiots are lit up like a bloody Christmas tree."

The scope in front of Georgia showed her that a large object was now racing towards them at high speed. She didn't even have time to warn Liam before the animal's front limb batted the little craft out of the way as it rushed towards the lights.

Something sharp smashed into Georgia's head. She heard an angry yell before darkness claimed her.

CHAPTER THREE

He snapped open his eyes to discover the severed head of the deputy warden. It was lying on his stomach while he lay in a mixture of sodden cardboard and small green apples. Maddock wrapped his fingers through the wet hair and slung the offending item out of his sight before slowly getting to his feet. He leaned against the bulkhead while waiting for the dizziness to pass. It took him a moment for his brain to catch up with the rest of his body and to fill him in on the events leading up to him finding himself in this state.

Maddock remembered those two goons pushing him inside this storage room. They left him in here with the door wide open, and Maddock frowned. That memory portion refused to show itself. Something disastrous had happened to the prison, that much was obvious. Not that he cared: it had saved him from a severe beating.

He certainly remembered those goons microwaving his muscles and the reason why they did it. Poor old Soapy Johnson. Still, it could have been worse; the sneaky little piece of human garbage might have gotten one on Maddock and stuck his shank in his thigh.

The deputy warden's pale eyes stared up at him from under the cold murky water. "You've lost a bit of weight since I last saw you." He kicked the head under the shelving so those accusing eyes would stop glaring at him. Like this was somehow his fault. "I know it's supposed to be wrong to speak ill of the dead, but let's face it, chump, you were a bit of a bastard."

He stretched out his arms and arched his back, feeling the bones crack. Having previous experience from recovering from their electro-batons, Maddock guessed that he'd been out for about an hour.

It then occurred to him that he shouldn't have been able to hear his bones crack. This was usually a noisy place, even after lights-out, when the prisoners were sleeping, the facility's ambient noise assured that the place was never truly silent. This place was as dead as the deputy warden. He splashed through the ankle-deep water, heading for the open doorway while wondering what had happened to the rest of his body.

There were bits of splintered timber floating along with the spilled apples. He guessed that's what happened to the door. He bent down and selected a long, thick piece. This would do as a makeshift weapon until he found something more appropriate. A dead guard carrying a gun would be ideal; failing that, a dead guard holding an electro-baton.

He had memorised most of the routes in this facility so he'd be able to reach the boats easily enough. That is, if he could get through the seemingly thousands of security gates. Even if he found a dead guard who had a key, it wouldn't work, not with the power out. In case of this happening, he assumed that the gate deadlocks would engage to make sure that no prisoner could do exactly what Maddock planned to do. The only officers who carried physical keys were the warden and deputy warden.

Maddock reached the doorway and peered out looking for either of the two men. What he saw made him silently thank the warden for appearing when he did. The man had inadvertently saved Maddock's life.

The corridor no longer existed, neither did half the room opposite. The walls and floor had gone; he guessed they had slipped into the water after all that violent shaking. Was it a quake, or had the facility been attacked? Whatever the reason, his journey towards those boats had now become a little more interesting and certainly wetter.

Cold Atlantic water now lapped at the edge of the doorway. There went his chance of taking the scenic route. Not that he needed the master key now. Good job considering their bodies were probably at the bottom of the ocean. All he had to do was swim under the gates.

He dipped the tip of his boot into the water then found himself shaking. Maddock dropped his club and grabbed the side of the door frame for support. His memory slotted the missing fragment back into place, giving him a front seat view of the creature which took the deputy warden after snapping off his head.

Maddock groaned. No way could that be right. He wasn't

exactly an animal expert, but even he knew that crocodiles longer than a great white only existed in those sea monster movies that he loved as a kid.

Even so, he couldn't deny what his eyes had showed him, not when that psychotic freak's severed head was still within kicking distance.

So where did that leave him? As far as he could see, Maddock would just have to take extra care while in the water. He picked up his club and choke back a laugh. Somehow, knowing that a monstrous Croc was stalking the facility made this look as effective as a tickling stick.

"I so need a gun." Maddock gazed across at what remained of the other room. It didn't look too promising. All he saw were piles of rubble and a couple of battered metal desks. It was in a room just like that where that man used to torture him, and he found himself wishing that the psycho hadn't died so quickly; he needed to suffer.

Maddock squinted his eyes. Was that a hint of blue that he noticed under all those rocks? He nodded to himself. Yes, he wasn't mistaken. That was a prison guard's uniform, he was sure of it. Maddock spun around and picked up three cans of tinned peaches and threw the first one across. The tin smacked against a roof beam before rolling into a corner. The second and the third exposed more clothing. He also caught sight of a leather holster. "Oh yes! Thank you. At last, some good news."

While he thought about how to get across without getting his feet wet, another chunk of masonry shifted, causing an avalanche of small stones to fall away from the corpse, revealing the dead man's face.

"Aw shit. Sorry, dude. You did not deserve that." The only decent screw lay under all that rubble. Donnie Maynard was a guy who played by the book; he didn't accept bribes and never turned his back while a couple of inmates beat the shit out of another prisoner. He wasn't a soft touch, no way. When he had to be, the man could be as hard as any other screw. He just understood that the guys in here were still human. Maddock turned and looked at the metal shelving bolted to the wall, wondering how easy that would come away.

He paused. Maddock didn't even know that the poor guy was dead. He turned and got as close to the edge as he dare. "Hey, are you okay over there?" There was no response. Not that he expected any. Still, if he had been out for almost an hour, then the other guy could be in the same condition. "Dude!" he shouted. "Is there anybody in there?"

Did he just see movement? Maddock grabbed the door-frame and leaned further out. Yes, there it was again, just by his leg - only it wasn't Maynard's leg which moved.

He watched in utter disgust and horror as a shiny black octopus the size of a dinner plate crawled out from the rubble, over the man's body, and fastened its legs tight around the guard's face. Another one scuttled out and joined its companion. This one fastened its slimy body directly over his ear. "Oi, get off him, you vile things!" he shouted.

Maddock's foot slipped, and he fell straight into the ice-cold water. Straight away, the octopuses left the dead man and slid over his body at high speed before dropping into the water.

He managed to climb back out before any of them got close. Maddock got to his feet, wondering what he was going to do now. This was insane. Since when did a bloody octopus become so aggressive? He considered throwing a few tins at them but then came up with a better solution. First, he needed to get across without entering the water. Maddock climbed over the sodden boxes, grabbed the shelving, and gave it a savage tug. He grinned in satisfaction when he felt it move.

After a couple more minutes of effort, Maddock had pulled a section of shelving away from the wall. He carried that over to the edge, leaned it against the wall then went back to collect something else. There were now six of the horrible things over there now. He kneeled down and splashed the water. Once again, the animals left the body and jumped into the water. It's obvious that they preferred their food to move. God, they were fast!

Before any of them could launch their clinging black bodies onto him, Maddock threw the severed head into the water, away from him. As soon as the animals changed direction, he dropped the metal shelving over the gap, picked up his club and ran across his bridge. Maddock hurriedly shifted the loose rocks around the guard's hip so he could claim his prize. He kept one eye on the gang of octopuses in the water while he pushed the rocks away. This really was turning into one strange day.

Once his prize was clear, Maddock took the belt, holster, and pistol as well as a few spare rounds that he found at the bottom of the holster. Now that he had something with a little more stopping power, he began to feel a little more relaxed; more in control. He stood over the body and drew the sign of the cross over his chest. It was a shame to leave him like this, at the mercy of those slimy, black fiends, but he had no other choice. Maddock still needed to find a way off this bloody rock. He also had to find his two cell mates. He couldn't leave them here, not if there really is some gigantic crocodile roaming through these waters.

Maddock gave the dead man one more respectful nod before he began to make his way over to the door. He then stopped dead. His instincts launched into overdrive. There was something behind him! He spun around, only to find another octopus climbing out of the guard's open mouth, its tentacles slapping against the corpse's skin while it pulled its soft body out of the hole. Maddock shook his head. "No, that's just not on." He brought up the gun, took off the safety, and fired a single shot into the middle of the black thing's body. "Rot in hell, you vile freak," he spat, before he ran over to the door.

He found himself back where he started from, near the elevator which led up to the compound. He wasn't going to get out that way, not with the power down. There were four other doors, and he knew for a fact that there was no way he'd be able to get through any of them, not without that key. Maddock was effectively trapped.

"Just great," he muttered. "I've escaped a beating from that psycho warden only to become octopus food." Maddock ran over to the elevator doors. It should be relatively easy to force those doors open if it was just the motor holding them shut. He needed a lever though, something strong or...

Maddock laughed softly; they always called him 'Mister Problem Solver' back when he was in the forces. Back in those days, it was more of a case of figuring out how to sneak out of base and hit the bars in town without getting caught.

He turned around and went to each door and checked them, something he should have done first. The one Maddock came through was left until the last resort. If he had no choice then he would have to go back where he started and drag that metal shelving into here, and without being eaten alive by a bunch of deranged octopus.

The last door opened as soon as he pulled the handle. His mad grin at finding another route out quickly fell off his face when he found he'd just opened a bloody store cupboard. Still, at least he now had a selection of possible tools that he could use to open those elevator doors. Maddock took out a broom that had a metal shaft, as well as a small shovel which he found at the back of the top shelf, hiding behind a can of polish.

Maddock laughed again when he pulled the shovel out, and a small bag of weed fell onto the floor. He pushed that into his back pocket. With his newly found items, Maddock returned to the elevator and discovered that the shovel edge fit nicely into the gap. With a bit of pressure, abuse language, and luck, he managed to open the doors enough to allow him to push his fingers inside, and with a couple of grunts, he pulled both doors open, showing him an excellent view of the elevator shaft.

"You have got to be kidding me," he muttered when he leaned inside. Like the room he'd just left, the lower levels had vanished, probably lying on the ocean bed a thousand feet below him. Maddock looked the other way and saw a rectangle of blue light about three floors up. It looked like somebody in the compound had opened the elevator doors at their end, and that gave him a cause to grin; it meant that somebody else still lived. I was beginning to think that I was the only one left.

Maddock leaned inside the shaft and found a recessed metal ladder, making his ascent so much easier. While trying to open the doors, he got the image of him having to shimmy up a metal rope like an incarnated Tarzan.

Maddock saw a recessed metal ladder in the middle of the shaft wall to his left. That would *so* make his ascent easier. While he was trying to force the doors open, he couldn't shift the image of him shimmying up a metal rope like Tarzan out of his mind. He knocked the sweeping brush end off the metal shaft and slid that through the belt before dropping his piece of wood on the floor. "Goodbye, wooden club. You were no use to me whatsoever."

He then counted to three before jumping across the water. His fingers instinctively curled around one of the ladder rungs. That sky-blue rectangle grew larger as he climbed. Maddock wanted to get up there as fast as possible, but dare not rush in case he slipped. His body still wasn't back to full strength. He reached the doors which led to the admin block and stopped to catch his breath. They all knew that the employees of Stone Yield prison had their own jetty as well as a couple of boats that were always ready to leave in case of any unexpected disaster. If this didn't fit into that category, he didn't know what did. Obviously, the boats were kept secured and under armed guard, but as he was now the new improved 'Mister Problem Solver', he didn't think their precautions would present much of a challenge. Besides, he now had a gun; if any of them gave him trouble, he could always shoot them.

A shadow passed over his arm and body. Maddock jerked his head up towards the elevator entrance just as a limp body plummeted past him and splashed into the water below. Maddock hooked his arm around the rung and pulled out the gun. There wasn't anybody else up there, even so, he doubted that the man just accidentally fell down the shaft.

He looked at the body, floating on the surface. He was face down so he couldn't recognise him. The man's body size did tell Maddock that it wasn't either of his cell mates, so it wasn't all bad. The man was definitely dead; the large hole in his neck and the copious amount of blood spilling into the water told him that much. Maddock wondered how long it would take for those octopuses to smell their next meal. Judging from his brief experience with them, probably a minute, perhaps less. In fact, there was some activity down there already. He saw something under the body, but it was no octopus, not unless they had suddenly grown.

Maddock pressed himself tight against the ladder and choke back a scream when a dark green head rose up from below and smashed against the insides of the shaft. The ladder that he hung onto groaned as the metal below Maddock twisted and buckled as that head full of nine inch serrated teeth continued to punch its bulk against the shaft in a desperate attempt to reach that body.

If he didn't move it, Maddock would end up down there, too; this ladder wasn't going to take much more punishment. While the ladder shook and bent, he raced up towards that light, so trying not to slip.

Two pairs of hands reached down and dragged his sweating body out seconds before the ladder was ripped from the wall. Maddock took a deep shaking breath before finding one of those arms savagely pushing him onto his back. The sun's bright glare didn't have time to burn his eyes before a huge mop of shaggy black hair blocked his vision.

"Ugh, I should have known you would have lived. Still, just means the Beast can do you himself. He's gonna have so much fun with you, Maddock."

While Donovan Bishop, the Beast's second in command, continued to explain in great detail what the prison's top dog would do to him, Maddock reached down his side, took out his gun, and casually pistol-whipped the idiot. Maddock got to his feet. "You talk too much."

He turned to find another prisoner facing him. This one had taken Maddock's metal stick.

"Blakey. What a coincidence. I was just thinking about you."

His cellmate grinned and offered the weapon back to Maddock who hand up his hands. "I wouldn't have let him do anything bad to you, honest. It's just that I was about to hit the goon when you cracked him with your gun. Say, where did you get that, and do you have one for me? God, am I glad to see you, Maddock." Blakey gave off his infamous nervous grin. "What's happening, man, and where did the sea dragon come from?"

He shrugged, "Search me. Does it matter? Look, have you seen Stix? We need to get off this rock. Sea dragon or not. When the authorities get wind of this, they'll come in here guns blazing. I don't want to be here when that happens."

Blakey nodded. "Sounds about right. Hang on." He grabbed Bishop's shoulders and dragged him towards the elevator shaft.

"What the hell are you doing?"

"Look, I see why you didn't shoot him, cos noise carries, but we can't let his cold black heart to continue pumping, not after what he's done. These fiends threw Constance down there just because he looked at Bishop in a funny way."

"Okay, you've convinced me." Not that it took much convincing. Bishop should have been executed. They had convicted him for the brutal murder of two kiddies. Bishop had claimed he had done lots more, but most inmates thought he only said that to look good in front of the Beast.

Maddock slipped the gun back and picked up Bishop's legs. Blakey had a point. They carried him over to the shaft and threw him down. "Right, now tell me where Stix is."

"I can do better than that," replied Blakey. "Come on, follow me, and keep the noise down! If they know you're here, they'll slaughter you."

The little man raced across the middle towards the compound's west wall. As they got closer, Maddock saw that somebody had found a way into the stores room, found a rope ladder, and used it to scale the fourteen-foot-high wall. Seemed like a bit of a stupid idea considering all that lay beyond the perimeter was a thousand miles of deep ocean.

Blakey scaled that ladder like some monkey and ran across that narrow wall. He followed after him, sighing when he saw the body of another prison guard lying beside the open store room door. Maddock had no idea who it was due to the man's head now resembling a smashed watermelon.

He raced after Blakey, painfully aware that one slip would see him ending his life in the same way as Soapy. The little man was at the end of the wall. He pulled Maddock down onto the rooftop.

"Nearly there," he whispered. "Get your popgun ready. You're gonna to need it."

He followed the little man's suggestion and took the gun back out of the holster. They both scurried on the flat roofs. It looked like their final destination was to be the watchtower and the far end. Maddock had no idea why they were going this way, but he didn't ask. Blakey obviously knew where he was going.

The little man grinned. "This is going to be so good. I can't wait to see the look on their faces when they watch their boss's face explode." He stopped and turned. "Please tell me that you'll take him out as soon as you see him?"

The man then pointed to the left and placed his finger against his lips. Blakey ran to the end of the roof and jumped over the edge. Maddock leaned over and saw Blakey lying on the floor frantically gesturing to him to get down. He looked up and saw why. There were five of them stood at on the edge of the roof just beyond the watchtower. He saw the Beast with two of the fiend 's lieutenants along with two prison guards.

He understood Blakey 's anxiety. If he could see them then they'd be able to see him, too, only they weren't looking in his direction. The sea, or more precisely what was in there, had fixed all of them to the spot.

Maddock climbed down and joined Blakey on the roof floor. He, like everybody else, stared in fascination at the creature in the ocean circling one of the prison warning buoys.

Christmas! Until now, he hadn't grasped the sheer size of the monster. It had to be the length of an articulated truck with that mouthful of so many teeth taking up a sixth of its length. It really did look like a dinosaur, except this one had paddle-like limbs, each one the size of a rowing boat. What shocked him more than any was the speed of it. The bastard could motor. It made him wonder if even if they did get off the rock in a boat, what's to stop that monster from chasing them and capsizing the boat?

"What are you waiting for? Plug the bastard!"

Maddock nodded. Blakey was right. Time was wasting. He took aim, but before he could fire, the pistol was snatched from his grasp. He rolled onto his back, and yet again, he found Bishop looming over him. This time, the bastard had Maddock's pistol.

He wiped water from his dripping face and grinned down at him. "Your plan to do me in didn't work. Looks like the monster had other plans." The man cocked the gun. "This really isn't your lucky day, is it?"

CHAPTER FOUR

After careful consideration, Fletcher Davis, otherwise known as The Prowler, decided to give his made up posthumous medal to the slimy little dog turd that he found shivering under a table in the laundry.

The Prowler didn't even know his name; all he knew about the fifty-something, balding man who smelled of rotting cheese was that of all the prisoners that he'd thrown into the tank was that his stamina had been superb. Cheeseman managed to last a full minute before The Prowler's new pet had gobbled him up.

"Arise Sir Screamalot, may your bones not get stuck in my new pet's throat and let's hope you don't give him stomach ache with your cheesy odour." He smiled to himself. That was funny. It's just a shame that there was nobody around to share his little joke.

Having nobody around him suited The Prowler just fine. He had spent most of his adult life avoiding other people. The Prowler preferred animals; he always had. Humans made him feel itchy and generally put him in a violent mood. The Prowler did not enjoy that combination. The only time when he could cope being around other people was when they slept.

The Prowler stroked the sides of the thick glass tank as he walked towards the exit. When people were just about to die was okay, too. In fact, he decided that he preferred that condition more than them being asleep, as when they were dead, they wouldn't be waking up.

He stood away from the tank and studied his reflection. The Prowler in front of him was smiling, something the real one never did. At least, not in here. Was he smiling, too? He pressed his fingers against the cold surface, watching his reflection do the same. "Reasons to be cheerful, part three."

The Prowler couldn't think of three reasons, but he had two, so that was a great start. He had found a new pet, which meant that for the first time since the evil bastards put him in here three months ago, he could finally end the grieving process for his beloved dog, Elbow. The apparent lack of other people qualified as his second reason – well, apart from the four he'd discovered while his travelled through the prison - but they didn't stay breathing for too long.

Yes, for the first time in three months, The Prowler was actually beginning to enjoy his life again. He stopped in front on the door which led upstairs and back into the prison's leisure complex and used the master key which he'd lifted from the deputy warden to unlock it. The prowler waited for the faint bleep before turning the handle.

Was it fate which led him to this point? In the past few hours since the disaster, he had wondered if some deity was watching over him, ensuring that The Prowler would be able to leave this dirty hell-hole and return to what he used to enjoy. How else could he explain his apparent compulsion to take the master key from the evil psycho when he was otherwise focussed on hating that other prisoner? During free-time, The Prowler generally stayed as far away as possible to all the other inmates as they all smelled funny and they had a tendency to call him names as well as hit him. The guards hit him as well, but he didn't mind that because while they used him as a punch-bag, on most occasions he was able to take stuff out of their pockets. Even so, him using his talents in the compound in full view of everyone was unheard of, and to take the master key, the one object which could lead him to freedom, too? Well, all he could say was The Prowler's balls must have been made of solid steel when he performed that incredible deed.

He glanced up at the low ceiling. Unless, that is, he had been somehow compelled to by God. In a way, it did make sense. After all, how else could he explain the sudden appearance of the beast? The real beast, the one in cell nine who went by that name. He was just some soulless demon wearing a coat of human meat.

He slowly walked up the metal steps. Oh, what he'd give to find that one and feed him to the real beast. Now that event would be worth watching. Only that wasn't going to happen; the human beast wouldn't be found hiding under a table, it wasn't his way. Besides, The Prowler already knew where he was.

So, was he the chosen one? Was he like Moses, but instead of leading the people out of Egypt, he was leading them into the mouths of his new pet? Again, this made sense as well for of all the people on this planet. He could think of no other group of low-life scum who deserved to be fed to the giant monster than these prisoners who, if they could, would abuse him and beat him up. Also, the prison guards, if he found any, would end up as food for the beast too. They were just as bad.

Perhaps if he did find another person, maybe his pet might come back? He had left the tank quite a while ago now, and The Prowler had, at the time, wondered if he had done something wrong. All that changed when he had a quick scout around the facility and found evidence that his pet had munched on a few other prisoners. While prowling, he came across two left hands, a foot, and a skull. The Prowler had even picked up the skull, believing that it was a fake. All that changed when some grey jelly-like stuff slivered out of the hole in the base of the skull and landed on his foot.

He might have screamed at that moment; The Prowler couldn't quite remember. He did remember seeing something black and shiny slither around a corner, and he also certainly remembered fleeing the area and making his way back here. It took him a good ten minutes to regain his composure and to continue his search.

After finding another foot floating in the water, it became obvious that the reason why his pet had left him was because some prisoners must have decided to swim to freedom. The fact that they were on an artificial island a thousand miles from the mainland obviously hadn't put them off. Most of them weren't very bright. Violent and unpredictable, oh yeah, they all had that in spades, but brains were hard to come by in here. The Prowler then thought of that skull. Yes, brains was one valuable commodity in this prison.

The beast would show up again; that much The Prowler did know. All he had to do was find out where all the other prisoners were congregating. The monster was bound to gravitate towards the largest group; it was only natural for it to head the largest food source.

He now felt so much better. Knowing that his pet couldn't be too far away even helped him get over his shock of finding that skull and that uneasy feeling that the beast wasn't the only unexpected visitor to the prison. The Prowler decided to put that nasty experience to the back of his mind and instead focussed on his primary objective of getting off this rock before the next visitor showed up. He knew for certain that the next visitors would be human in helicopters carrying high powered rifles and ready to shoot anyone in a prison uniform. The Prowler intended to be far away from here when that happened.

"I suppose I had better make tracks." He waved goodbye to the prison's swimming pool for the last time and left the leisure suite. It made him smile to think that the pool only lasted a week before they shut it down permanently. It appeared that none to the idiots who came up with the ridiculous idea of installing a pool in a high security facility thought that it wouldn't be abused. It turned out that prisoner 32453, formally known as Squeak, became its first and only victim. The official report stated accidental drowning, but everybody knew that there hadn't been anything accidental. Squeak owed the Beast two lunch tokens and a pair of boots. As he refused to pay up, he paid with his life.

The Prowler heard that three prisoners watched him try and learn to be a fish via the huge glass partition on the floor below. The very same partition where he watched his pet eat the prisoners. He couldn't swim to the surface due to belts tied to his arms and legs and bolts stolen from the workshop stuffed in his pockets.

Thanks to his master key, he made swift progress through the prison interior, keeping a close eye out for anything capable of stripping flesh from a skull and sucking out the brains. Something weird, black and shiny. The Prowler shivered, not altogether sure if he wanted to know what else was in here besides him. At least his pet stayed in the water.

He hurried past the staff canteen, noting more movement over by one of the metal counters, but didn't hang about to see what it was. The Prowler needed to find the others. He only slowed down and stopped when he reached a nondescript door, hidden in a corner. As far as he knew, the janitors stored their cleaning supplies behind that door, meaning that there might even be a change of clothing. The prowler was confident that he'd get away from the rock, but in case that didn't happen, then the last thing he needed to look like would be a prisoner. Even he didn't think they'd shoot a janitor. The thought of him disguised as a janitor did make him smile. It was almost as absurd as him dressing up in a biblical grey dress and leading the prisoners to his pet. Come to mention it, that notion was ridiculous as well. His pet didn't need him to fetch food. The beast could do that well enough on his own. Of course, he could. Everything that moved in the water was potential dinner for his beautiful pet. Nothing could harm him. The Prowler knew this because he had developed a bond with the animal.

Ever since childhood, the young Fletcher Davis had the unnerving ability to understand other people's pets. It wasn't only domesticated animals either. His mum refused to take him shopping due to Fletcher's annoying knack for having dozens of pigeons following him everywhere.

His mum always used to say that the animals would get him into trouble one day. The old bat's prophetic words were actually at the forefront of his mind when that judge handed him his sentence. The Prowler was just thankful that she wasn't around any more to witness her eldest son getting carted away for a punishment which didn't fit the crime. Not to his eyes anyway.

He specialised in house breaking. In fact, he was famous for it. He had become so famous that the national media had even chosen his new name. Fletcher actually liked his new name. His infamy came to an abrupt end three months ago when, on one miserable Thursday winter evening, he broke into a huge property complete with the top of the range alarm system as well as trained attack dog. At least, that's what it said on the warning sign outside the gated property. The Prowler had no fear of either. Sales from his ill-gotten gains had paid for certain software which made any alarm system utterly useless. As for attack dogs, is unique ability turned any vicious canine into a playful drooling puppy.

After disabling the alarms, The Prowler entered the house via the door at the rear, scrambling over two high fences, and picking the lock. As soon as the warm air hit him, he sensed that the owner had not gone to bed like he was supposed to. He could hear the sounds of what sounded like a kinky sex game. Plenty of whipping with a few moans thrown in for good measure. He knew there and then that he should have left and come back at a later date, but his curiosity got the better of him. The Prowler silently sneaked through the house and walked in on the owner whipping his dog with a studded rope. The evil bastard had tied another length tight around the dog's muzzle to stop him howling.

He snatched the knotted rope out of the house owner's hands, and beat him to death with the offensive item. It took him a good hour to kill him, at least that's what he heard from the police later. He was still there when they arrived. They found him covered in the man's blood, cradling the sleeping dog while rocking back and forth.

The door swung open revealing nothing but an empty cleaning trolley and a couple of plastic bottles on the back of a wooden shelf. There were no uniforms. Still, it wasn't all bad news, as he did manage to locate a candy bar secreted inside a plastic pocket on the cleaning trolley.

Upon leaving the cupboard, The Prowler gravitated towards one of the offices opposite the staff canteen. Unlike the other doors he'd found, this was open. He peeked inside and smiled in delight when he saw a knife lying in the middle of the desk. It was similar to the one he always carried around with him whenever he went out on a job.

He grabbed it and slid the weapon inside his sock. It made him feel almost whole again. The Prowler turned towards the window and realised that he could feel the ocean breeze. Somebody had left the window open. No wonder there was a smile on his face. The smell around the staff areas wasn't so bad, unlike the prison blocks where the stink of all those unwashed bodies made him want to throw up almost every day.

The Prowler moved past the desk and gazed out of the window. "There you are," he whispered at the sight of the other inmates stood on the prison roof some distance away. He also felt the presence of his new pet, too. He couldn't see him, but the monster was close - very close.

He soon discovered how close when he saw the Beast push a prison guard off the edge of the roof. The guard shrieked as he plummeted, which were abruptly cut off when The Prowler's pet leapt out of the water and caught the falling man in those huge jaws.

His razor sharp serrated teeth sliced through skin, muscle, fat, and bone, reducing that guard into several morsels of tasty man food with one bite. He clapped in appreciation before, reluctantly, turning away. They had one more guard up there but The Prowler knew they wouldn't throw him over. No, they'd need that man to help them got off the rock.

They'd head for the jetty and use the boat to get as far away from here as possible. It's what he'd do. Once they were clear, then they'd sacrifice the guard to the monster. He might not like a single member of his species, but it didn't mean he couldn't predict their actions. After all, humans were animals, too.

He was going to make sure that before they left the rock that an additional passenger would be on board. Namely him. He turned away from the window and raced out of the office. Unbeknownst to those fools, he knew that if he didn't stowaway, that boat wouldn't last five minutes. His pet wouldn't attack it with him on board.

CHAPTER FIVE

It took Georgia a full five minutes to realise that Liam had removed her bra while she'd been out. When she challenged him, the young man didn't look the least bit bothered that he'd encroached upon her body without her consent. He simply pointed to the repaired rip in the craft's bulkhead, stating that he did what he had to in order to keep them alive. A couple of minutes later, after he had finally got the engines to start, Liam did admit that he had to use his socks, too; like that made what he did perfectly acceptable.

She saw no sign of that nightmarish monster, thankfully. She didn't want to ask him if it was still around. She couldn't see the installations, either. Where were they?

"How's the head?"

Georgia tentatively felt the side of her head where the first aid box had hit her. One day, maybe in a couple of weeks time, Georgia will find this utterly hilarious. Right now, all she wanted to do was to have a bit of a cry in private, preferably without this throbbing pain. Still it could be worse; she didn't think there was any lasting damage. No concussion or anything. Liam had done a fabulous job with the dressing. Even so, he still insisted on getting her to the doctor as soon as they docked. "I'm just a little sore," she replied. "Where are we?"

"The currents took us a couple miles away. Don't worry. It won't take long to get back now that I've fixed the engines.

"Good, because you're still buying me a drink, Liam. You're not going to wriggle out of it."

"Once we get you checked out, I promise I'll buy you a drink."

His reply did not exactly fill her with excited anticipation. Maybe she was reading too much into his response and body language. It felt as though she'd woken up to find Liam had developed a completely different personality. Georgia stared hard at the man. Something was wrong here, *really* wrong.

"Liam?"

"He turned around."

"Tell me what you saw?" she asked quietly. "When I was knocked out. Tell me what happened here."

He stayed silent for another minute. Georgia honestly believed that he wasn't going to answer her.

"I took the machine to the surface before fixing you up. I then got to work on the leak." Liam took a deep breath. "I guess I should be thankful for the job as it stopped me from looking out of the port windows."

Liam now looked like he'd just seen the world explode.

"Have you looked up yet, Georgia?"

She frowned, wondering why he'd ask such a weird question. Nevertheless, she did as he bid. The surface was a good thirty feet up. Her frown grew deeper. They were travelling under a dark shadow; it looked like an oil tanker had spilled its load into the water. "What is it?"

"It's blood," he replied. "Lots and lots of blood. That dinosaur of yours had been busy. It's decimated the local wildlife in the space of a few hours. Is that what this thing does?"

"Who can say?"

"I was hoping you could, Georgia. After all, as of right now you are the closest thing we have to an expert. Tell me everything you know about your Liopleurodon."

"You remembered its name!"

"I never forgot it."

"To be honest, Liam, there's very little anybody knows about the creature. After all, apart from a few fossilised bones, we have little else to go on. Still, I'll give it my best shot. We believe that it was the apex predator due to us not finding any other creature larger. Most believe that they were lone hunters and not pack animals like lions or wolves."

"Because of their size?"

She nodded. "The ocean doesn't have enough resources to feed too many predators. The skill it showed earlier does confirm that, too. It reminded me of a moray eel in the way it launched out of the galleon"

"How does that explain the bits of fish floating above us?"

She shrugged. "I don't have all the answers, Liam, although I do have one theory, but you better hope that I'm wrong"

Liam adjusted the course setting. "We're almost back," he said. "We'll be within visual range in a minute." Liam turned. "So, come on. Don't leave me suspense. Keep talking!"

"Back in the Jurassic and Cretaceous periods, there were no aquatic mammals. No dolphins, no seals, and definitely no whales. Our Liopleurodon hunted other predators. Other plesiosaurs, sharks, and Icthyosaurs would have been its main diet." She grinned at him. "See if you can guess what happens if you dump a bucket full of lumps of meat and blood into the water where there's sharks close by."

"No. No way. Are you saying that they go fishing? That's ridiculous."

"I'm not saying anything. It's just the evidence fits the facts. It could be right above us even as we speak, hiding amongst all that , and waiting for some unwary shark to come and have a nosey."

"If what you say is true then this is just unbelievable."

"No, not really. It's just another animal that's found an edge over its competitors. Although it is a worry. It shows some degree of planning; an intelligence. I'm not saying that they are brainy enough to solve complex equations or anything, but it does mean that until it's caught, any living creature in this ocean is it risk. Hell, it could even pose a hazard to the shipping lanes."

"Bloody hell."

"Did you hear anything else from the resort?"

"That's something I was going to talk to you about, Georgia." He nervously licked his lips. "You see, I can't get in contact with the resort."

"The radio was probably damaged in the turbulence, Liam. Don't worry about it." Her calming words didn't assure him; Georgia saw that right away. "Wait, it's not the radio?"

He shook his head. "Our radio works fine, and so does the one at their side." He sighed again. "It's just that nobody is answering." He applied more pressure on the control stick, accelerating the little craft. "It's probably nothing. We'll find out soon enough, lady. There's the galleon, and I think I can see the first observation bubble."

She inwardly cringed when he steered the craft past the galleon, expecting the Liopleurodon to launch out from within the installation's murky depths, its jaw open to the maximum, ready to crunch down on the fragile outer casing. Georgia wrapped her arms tight around her body so Liam wouldn't notice her shivering. She also bitterly cursed her active imagination. Not that any of the abuse did her any good, not when the water cleared so she could clearly see the resort's outer walls and the several observation bubbles. "Where's the lights? There should be lights."

She heard a low humming. Georgia didn't realise the noise was coming from Liam until she looked directly at him. He pushed the control stick even further forward. The little craft tilted down for a brief second until the inertia kicked in. They lurched forward, getting closer and closer to the resort. Most detail became clear, and it soon became obvious why they couldn't see any light in any of the observation bubbles. It was partly because several of them were no long there. Georgia's stomach knotted up, knowing full well that most of the people in there were now probably dead.

The guts of the resort, the inner workings - the guest rooms, bars, restaurants, crew cabins - were all below sea level. Only the few leisure facilities, main greeting lounge, and heliport were above ground.

Liam slowed the craft and stopped it directly in front of where the closest observation bubble used to be. Tears streaked down Georgia's face at the sight of the single human body lying under a toppled bookcase. Several yellow fish danced around the dead man's exposed hand, nibbling away his finger flesh. They all scattered when Liam activated the front lights.

Just for a couple of seconds, she spotted more movement. Something black and shiny slid off the man's ankle and vanished behind the bookcase. Georgia didn't even want to think about what it had been.

"Oh, God," she whispered. "It must have rammed the bubble!" A few small shards of thick concave glass were embedded in the dead man's stomach and neck. "He will have watched the monster racing towards him." She looked at Liam. "Why didn't he get out of there?"

"Why would he? You said it yourself, Georgia. He was probably off his head on expensive drugs. The daft old fool might have even thought that the monster was part of the attractions. Come on. We had better see if we can find a way inside."

There was something different about the man sitting beside her. It took her a moment to pin it down. Despite the horror, the death, and the possible prospect of both of them ending up like that poor bastard they'd just trundled past, she believed that Liam was actually enjoying all of this. Was her twisted imagination playing tricks on her again? How could anybody become excited at facing possible death?

"We ain't going to be able to dock in our usual spot, that's for sure. Well, we will, but there's no chance of getting out of the craft." Liam chuckled. "Not unless you can hold your breath for twenty minutes. I'll take her into the submerged corridor, the one which leads up to the grand staircase. Maybe we can find to route to the surface that way?"

She acted the quiet, terrified passenger as Liam expertly manoeuvred the machine through the smashed observation bubble and into the narrow passage, biting her bottom lip when the top left side brushed against a light fitting.

Liam leaned forward and looked through the top of the curved window. "Oh, that doesn't look good."

"What's wrong? Is the route blocked?"

"No, not at all. It's just that it might be a little bumpy from now on. I think you'd better close your eyes, and keep them shut until I say otherwise."

"What? I'm not going to do that. You can't treat me like child."

"Suit yourself," he replied. Liam pulled back on the control stick, and the craft rose towards the ceiling.

She saw the huge hole that he was heading towards. Georgia also saw why he asked her to close her eyes. The hole was not a natural phenomenon. Something had chewed through the thick floor boards, turning the wood into tiny pieces of splintered timber which floated through the water. Georgia choked back a low moan of horror when she finally worked out where they were and why he asked her to close her eyes. Liam had taken the craft into the resort's finest area containing two casinos, several exclusive restaurants, a theatre, and a ballroom.

The submersible floated directly under the ballroom, and from what drifted from the ballroom, she now knew where their rich guests must have been when this section began to flood. A severed hand, still attached to its forearm, bumped against the glass canopy as Liam began to move towards the large hole. When the limb hit the glass, an expensive gold watch slipped off the wrist, and sank into the murky depths below.

"Oh Jesus." Georgia slammed palm of her hand against her mouth.

"Close your eyes," he repeated.

She shook her head. "No, not this time. It doesn't feel right, like it's disrespectful."

"Lady, if you want to go all spiritual on me, just think of their bodies as empty shells; that their souls have already left for a better place. It's just unfortunate that your Liopleurodon had to bite them in half so their souls could leak out."

"You really need to lighten up, Georgia. For crying out loud, so a bunch of rich jerks got eaten by an extinct sea monster. So what? It's what they all deserved anyway."

"That's just horrible. I can't believe you just said that you sick freak."

"While I'm on the subject of lighting up..."

He leaned forward and activated the front lights. Twin beams picked out bits and pieces of shredded flesh as hundreds of tiny fish obscured the pieces of meat. She tried not to imagine what had gone through their panicking minds when that water started to rise. The lights swept along one of the walls, and Georgia spotted long, dark fabric drapes hanging down from the balcony.

Some of them would have scrambled up those, desperately trying to get as high as possible.

How many of them had tried to climb up those drapes, in a desperate attempt to escape the rising sea water? How many had been kicked off the drapes by the ones already at the top?

He said that they all deserved what had happened to them. Could she even agree? After all, no matter how abhorrent they were to each other and to the people who served them, even they didn't deserve their eventual fate.

The craft neared the ceiling, and just like she predicted, there were bits of human flesh right at the top as well. Georgia so wanted to cry.

The deafening sound coming from below would have caused every one of those remaining survivors to scream with terror. Their survival instinct wouldn't have allowed any of them to let go, to uncurl those freezing fingers from around that sodden fabric, even as the inevitable hit them. Even while the water continued to rise, they would have carried on clinging to the drapes, right up to the point where that leviathan rose out of the cold water, and fastened its tusk-like front teeth around their legs and dragged them, shrieking into the ocean.

"Why did you turn on the lights, Liam?"

"I need to see where I'm going, that's why!" he snapped. "Besides, what part of close your eyes did you not understand?"

"Don't you have any sympathy for what happened in here?"

"No, not one bit. I told you, they were all just parasites. It really couldn't happen to a nicer bunch of people. Now, are you going to shut up, or do I have to slap you?"

"You touch me, you bastard and I'll..."

"You'll what, lady? Scream for help? Because that will work. I bet that will bring all the policemen in their police submarines rushing to help their damsel in distress."

Georgia curled both her hands into tight fists, ready to hit him in the balls if he did try anything. God, how stupid had she been? To think that she had fancied this creep. Oh shit, he'd taken her bra off as well!

It took her another couple of moments for her to realise that the pig next to her had stopped the craft. Georgia peered through the front window, trying to make out what she was looking at. He'd made it difficult by dimming the lights. Had they stopped in front of the ballroom ceiling? What was he playing at? The woman turned to face him, intending to tell this man exactly what she thought of him.

Her harsh words just fell away when she saw the look of total despair plastered across the man's face. Where had the cruel sneer and those mocking eyes gone to?

"How do you feel?" he asked softly.

Liam reached for her, and she instinctively backed away. "Don't you dare touch me," she hissed.

"As a species, we're not too competent at handling more than one extreme emotion at once. While you were being furious with my despicable behaviour, I managed to fly you straight through the worst of the mess." He shrugged. "I'm so sorry, Georgia, but I couldn't think of anything else to do when you refused to close your eyes."

"Wait. You mean?" she furiously wiped away her tears, the penny had already dropped. "Just tell me where we are."

"The designers built in several safeguards to this facility in case of any potential disaster. They had to account for any possible accident in order to satisfy the hordes of reps that the insurance companies sent. Granted, not one of them came up with 'what happens if a prehistoric monster attacks the resort', but even so, they did include countermeasures for the resort filling up with water."

Liam pointed ahead. "That's our way out, Georgia."

"Sorry, you've lost me. What countermeasures? Nobody told me about any safeguards apart from the usual ones."

"I know. Just like the administrators decided in their infinite wisdom to keep it from becoming public knowledge. They believed that if the visitors became aware, they wouldn't come, thinking the resort to be unsafe, that it could sink to the bottom of the Atlantic at any moment. The only reason I know is because I've been here since it opened."

That is a hatchway which opens out onto the floor above. I'm hoping that isn't flooded as well. I don't think it will be; I think we're pretty close to sea level."

Georgia saw it now. The circular pattern in front of them wasn't just a fancy decoration at all. How could she have not noticed it before? More to the point, why hadn't anybody else said anything? Liam couldn't be the only person here who knows of this.

"Sea water gushing into the resort was one of their concerns. Hence the reason for the escape hatch. In theory, all the trapped people had to do was to keep afloat until the level reached the ceiling, open the hatch, and escape."

"So how do we open it without getting our feet wet?"

He smiled at her. "I've already linked the Nautilus to the mechanism. Watch."

Three square buttons in the middle of the hatchway blinked on, giving the surrounding area a deep red tinge. It reminded Georgia of blood. She attempted to shake away the disturbing imagery which eagerly followed it, but her bitter imagination refused to play ball. She saw all her newly enlightened guests swimming towards those blinking red lights, only to find themselves being pulled under the water one by one by the monster. By the time the hatched opened, there'd be nobody left to climb to safety, and if there was anybody up there waiting, all they'd see when the hatch opened would be dark seawater.

"Are you okay? It's just that you're shaking."

He placed his hand on her knee, and this time she didn't push him away. "Liam, that hatch looks rather small. Will this craft fit through it?"

"No," he replied. "Just the forward section. Once that's through, our front canopy will swing open, allowing us to climb out. They've thought of everything. Don't worry."

"But what if the next level is flooded too?"

"It won't be."

"But what if it is?"

"Then I'll have to make you angry with me again."

"I don't think it will work a second time."

"There you go. Look, the hatch is opening."

The complete sense of relief which Georgia felt when that hatch slid away to reveal that the water hadn't flooded the next level almost crashed her system.

"Can I have my hand back, please?"

Georgia snatched her own hand away. She hadn't even realised that she'd put it on top of his. Four deep crescent shaped marks were clearly visible. "Sorry about that."

He shrugged. "No bother. Look, you can have the hand back in minute. I just need it right now." Liam's fingers danced across the control panel. "You can relax now, lady. The worst part is over. There should be a few people who've survived. There's probably a whole fleet of rescue helicopters already on the way."

She watched the little craft dock onto the hatchway. Georgia thought she was going to cry again when the submersible's glass canopy broke the surface. There was nobody about, but that didn't matter. The place was dry. Several short arms extruded from the edges, swung down, and clamped the craft tight.

"Okay, wait here. I'll just make sure it's safe."

"Why won't it be safe?"

"Who knows? Look, please sit tight just for a second." Liam suddenly leaned across and kissed her lightly on the cheek."

"What was that for?"

"For putting up with me, I guess. Most people generally keep their distance." He unbuckled himself then pressed a couple more buttons.

The canopy lifted up, and warm sea air rushed in. After breathing in the recycled stuff for all those hours, the clean air caressing her slick skin felt like the second-best thing that had happened to her today. "Ye Gods. I so need a shower."

"You can have one as well as a drink once we're away from here." Liam climbed out of the machine and crawled up onto the metal gantry. "Strange. I thought somebody would be here." He stood up and arched his back.

She didn't want to stay here any longer. The cool air had made her clothing stick to her sweaty body. Georgia looked past Liam and took in her surroundings. They weren't in any place she knew. It made her realise just how little she knew about the place where she'd lived, worked, and slept for the last two years. Hell, Georgia had made it her mission to ensure that not one piece of this resort would stay concealed from her eyes.

Looks like she had missed a bit.

Georgia frowned when she felt something bump against the Nautilus. That frown turned in an audible yelp when the craft suddenly lurched. "Liam!" she yelled. "Get back here, right now!" Georgia moaned in utter terror when the tortured sound of shearing metal reached her ears. The craft lurched again.

Her shaking fingers fumbled with the seat buckle. All around her, the craft's interior buckled and tore. The shaking grew more violent. "Liam, please help me!" Why couldn't she work her fingers? The buckle mechanism flat out refused the budge.

A hand suddenly grabbed the front of the belt while Liam sliced through the strong fabric with a double-edged blade. Before he could reach for the other strap, three more clamps were wrenched off. Liam was thrown back into the cockpit, and his knife went flying.

She reached for the man, totally forgetting she was still strapped in. The last clamp fell away. Georgia knew exactly what was happening, and she also knew that if she didn't get her shit together, they'd both end up dead.

"I'm not going to die without my drink, Liam," she growled. Seeing him in trouble gave Georgia the clarity of thought needed to focus on the job which previously seemed impossible. She unbuckled herself, reached down, and grabbed Liam's wrist before she pulled herself and the man out of the craft just as it gave one final crunch, and fell from the hatchway.

Georgia dragged him onto the metal gantry. "Get up, for Christ's sake, Liam. Move it!"

The man got to his feet just as a wall of cold water crashed into the pair of them, knocking Georgia onto the floor. She got back onto her knees and spun around to see the huge reptile's nightmarish head snap forward. Its jaws opened and closed around Liam's ankles then pulled him into the water.

CHAPTER SIX

Back in his younger days, when Maddock sincerely believed that nothing could kill him, he had a mate who once told him that if he ever found himself facing the business end of a gun, the only honourable response was to laugh at the bastard whose finger was on the trigger.

That had sounded like some surefire way of having your head blown off. Then again, his mate had never been all that smart. He'd often wondered what had happened to Liam with his funny little ways and his obsession with the sea.

There wasn't a chance in hell that laughing at Donovan Bishop would result in anything less than Maddock's mushed brains leaving the back of his skull, but that didn't mean he shouldn't adapt and modify his mate's old piece of advice. He allowed hint of a smirk to play across his mouth. "Dude, if you're going to pull that trigger, you might want to take the safety off first. You know, just saying."

It was inevitable that the greasy shit stain's eyes would move to the side of the weapon he'd just snatched. The momentary break in concentration was all Maddock needed. He launched his left foot up, striking the small collection of soft objects between the man's legs with great force. Maddock rolled out of the way as the groaning man dropped to his knees.

Bishop's finger tightened. Maddock saw a tiny spark of realisation of being duped appearing behind all those waves of pain rolling through the prisoner's body when the gun killed a lump of concrete.

Maddock got to his feet and retrieved his property.

"You're a complete tool, Bishop," he spat, before hitting him with his gun again. This time Maddock made sure that The Beast's second in command wouldn't be getting up anytime soon. He pulled Blakey up. "We'd better start moving. This idiot's boss will be sending some more clowns to investigate."

"Maybe not. I mean, he'd probably think a guard just shot a

prisoner of something or that Bishop's just killed you and me. He won't risk breaking up his people." Blakey nodded. "Yeah, he won't come looking for us."

Maddock grabbed the wet man's feet and dragged him closer to the edge. He'd already seen that his intended targets had made themselves scarce. That was a shame but not altogether surprising. The Beast was no fool. He leaned over, took Bishop's arms, and pulled them towards him.

"What are you doing?"

"Isn't it obvious?" Maddock wrapped his fingers around the railing then rolled the unconscious man over the edge. He waited for the splash before nodding in satisfaction. "There, come back from that."

Blakey joined him at the railing. They both started when the sea dragon leapt out of the sea and took the offering before disappearing back under the surface. Maddock looked straight at his cellmate.

"Blakey, I want them to come looking for us, and hopefully in small groups. They're much easier to kill that way." He ejected the clip and pressed down on the 'W' spring. "An M1911. I had one like this, you know, a long time ago. She saved my life on a few occasions."

"She? Wait, you named her?"

"Sure, I did. Jennifer and I were good mates for years." He pushed the clip back into place. Maddock just hoped that they'd be able to find some more ammo for his new mate before he ran out. Four bullets weren't going to get him right far.

"Are you going to name this one?"

"Shut up, Blakey." Maddock had no desire to kill anyone else, either guard or fellow prisoner. The only urge which drove him involved finding some way off this rock before the armed response units flew in. The blood lust he saw in Blakey's beady little eyes suggested that his shifty cellmate wouldn't be satisfied with just escaping. He saw this disaster as the ideal opportunity to exact revenge on those who had done him harm in the years that he'd been banged up. Unfortunately, due to his diminutive size and obvious non-threat status, he'd been used as a punch bag by a huge amount of the prison population. Blakey wouldn't be happy until he'd killed everybody who so much as looked at him funny. Normally, Maddock would have just told him to suck it up, to be satisfied that he had a friend to watch his back as well as to help him get that miserable hide away from here.

Normality did not apply to their situation. For starters, The Beast wanted Maddock's head on a stick, and just like Blakey, the bastard held grudges. And just like Maddock's cellmate, he'd rather find some way of achieving the separation of Maddock's head from his body before actually escaping.

As for the sea dragon, well, he didn't even want to start applying his meagre brain juice on how to deal with that thing.

"They shouldn't have had guns on them," said Blakey. "At least not in the compound; not near the like of us." I hope I can find a gun. If not a gun, I'd settle for a taste. Here, you reckon a taste would sort out the sea dragon?"

Maddock hoped that the man's dice with death might have shut him up for a few minutes. He just shrugged then went back to the ledge and walked the perimeter, looking for a way down. "Blakey, how did the others get out of the compound; did they get away before the power went down?" That sounded the most logical. They could have jumped a guard and forced the poor bugger to let them out or face certain death, even knowing that they probably would be killed even if they did help. The urge to keep breathing no matter the odds was always a great motivator.

"I don't really know. I mean, like I know they got off, but can't rightly remember how."

"What do you mean you can't remember. Don't give me that. Either you do or you don't." He then glanced towards the spot where he'd rolled Bishop into the water. "Okay, so what happened. Why were you, Bishop, and Zack left behind?"

"Do you know what I'm in for?"

"Sure. You never stop telling me and Stix about the hidden cache of notes that your buddies hid after the heist." Blakey had been the one to crawl through two miles of sewer and the van's ventilation shafts, leaving behind little packages of explosives.

The subsequent detonations paralysed the local traffic grid as well as the bank security system. The explosions also caused the deaths of three women and a seven-year-old girl, hence the life sentence. The rumours were that the police found him hiding in a tunnel, covered in rotting human excrement.

"The Beast ordered those two to stay behind and to find the location of the money despite the fact that I'd been locked up when the others hid it." He grinned crooked. "Don't know what them two did; I kept my gob shut. "Didn't get anything but insults."

"That's great. I'm happy for you. Now tell me how they got out."

"They scarpered before the gates locked up. One of the guards owed The Beast a favour."

This meant that the chances of either of them leaving now was reduced from slim to impossible. Hell, they couldn't even jump over the edge. Maddock climbed back onto the roof above. He wished his cellmate would try his best to keep the bullshit levels down to a bare minimum when he was around Maddock. The guy did himself no favours. He walked over to the edge and leaned over, aware that Blakey was right behind him. His bullshit meter had not gone down, and he'd just figured out why. Maddock spun around, grabbed the unsuspecting man by the shoulders, and swung him around.

"What are you doing, man? I ain't done anything to you. Let me go!"

"Are you sure you want me to do that?" Maddock released one hand then gagged him again when Blakey screamed. "How were you and Bishop getting off the roof? Come on, no more lies, Blakey. Tell me the truth." The sea dragon had returned. It made him wonder if it knew that there could be a meal up above or if its arrival was just a coincidence.

"Come on, stop trying to think up another lie, Blakey. My arm is getting really tired. Oh, and your pal is back. Swimming in a circle, right under you." He jerked his arms down a fraction, and a grim smile of satisfaction appeared on Maddock's face when he screamed again.

"It's the stress points, Maddock!" he shouted. "The concrete's the reason why. Oh, God, don't drop me; please I don't want to be eaten."

He pulled the weeping man away from the edge. "Okay, tell me what you're talking about, and don't lie to me. If I think you are telling porkies, I will throw you over." Maddock felt like a complete shithead for putting Blakey through that, but he couldn't think of any other way. Christ, why couldn't the man just tell the truth?

Blakey dropped to the floor and took in a few deep breaths. "I think I almost pissed my pants." he looked up. "You wouldn't have really dropped me, would you?"

"What is it with you and lying, man.? For crying out loud. Why didn't you just come out with that in the first place? Hell, it would have saved us so much pissing about."

I didn't know," he said. "Man, I wanted to, but I just kinda opened my mouth and told you whatever I thought you wanted to know. " Blakey sighed loudly. "I just wanted to please you, man. I don't know."

"Well, you can please me now by telling the truth, so talk to me, Blakey."

He sighed. "Okay, it's simple. Whatever happened to the prison has caused far more damage than it should due to the inferior composition of the materials used in its construction. There's hairline fractures and spider cracks everywhere. I really believe that if this place suffers another tilt like the last one, the whole prison will break apart. I bet they cut loads of corners when they built the damn place. Makes sense really. Christ knows how much it must have cost to transport all the gear they needed a thousand miles into the middle of the Atlantic."

"Wait, so how does this help us exactly?"

"It means that we don't have to get to wherever we're going via any normal route. All we need to do is find a weak part of the material and hit the concrete with something hard. The stuff will literally crumble like compressed flour, trust me."

He didn't trust Blakey as far as he could throw him, but what he said did make sense. Also, Maddock couldn't think of any other way out. "Okay, so tell me how you know all of this?"

"We all have our own particular skill, Maddock. Listen to me. Did you think the people who successfully pulled off that heist hired me for my good looks and charm?" The man slowly got to his feet. "Besides, I've also tested the concrete. That stuff they've used really is poor quality."

"We'd better get back then, hadn't we, Blakey?" Maddock hurried over to the wall. Before he climbed up, he looked over his shoulders. "To answer your question, buddy, the answer is no, of course, I wouldn't have dropped you." He paused, waiting for the man to smile. "That doesn't mean you couldn't have slipped through my fingers."

There could be something he might be able to use in that work-shed they passed earlier. Maddock still wasn't totally sure that he could trust the man, but unless he fancied going back down that lift shaft what choice did he have? Even if he did go back the way he came, Maddock wouldn't be able to go anywhere else. He'd be back where he started and trapped with only a severed head and a bunch of hungry octopuses to keep him company.

He ran along the wall and shimmied down the rope ladder. Maddock waited until Blakey was down before he pulled the rope down and rolled it up. He looped that over his head then walked over to the shed and peered inside. Sure enough, there was a hammer lying on a wooden shelf next to a box of nails and a screwdriver. Maddock took everything and distributed the stuff around his body.

"Right, it's time for you to show me one of these stress points." Maddock passed Blakey the hammer. "Let's get out of here."

"Gladly. There's a big one right by the west stand where the Maynard brothers used to congregate. We'll check that out first. It's the one I showed to Bishop."

Maddock put his hand on the man's shoulder, expecting him to flinch. Blakey stopped and looked behind him.

"Is this the part where you say that you're sorry?"

"I guess so."

"Don't have to. I know why you did it, and I guess I'd have done the same in your situation. Now, let's put that unpleasantness behind us. After all, we still have to get Stix away from those animals."

Maddock's bullshit meter jumped to alarming levels again, but this time he put a blanket over it, and blamed it on his already frayed nerves. "After you, Blakey." He let go of the man's shoulder and followed him across the empty compound. As he ran, Maddock thought back to his old buddy, Liam, and wondered what ever happened to him. They lost touch with each other years back, both going their separate ways. Whatever he was doing, it had to be far better than trying to escape from the high security prison.

Then again, thinking back to what he used to be like, the maniac would be enjoying every minute of it. He thrived on the danger; the more of it, the happier he was. Admittedly, back in the day, Maddock thrived on it, too. But back then they only had to deal with other humans. At no time had any of their training covered giant sea monsters and aggressive flesh eating octopuses.

"Blakey, this is going to sound like an odd question, but what is the plural for octopus?"

"Yeah, you're right, it is an odd question. Stix will know; he's the one who does the crosswords."

He stopped beside the metal stand. Blakey spun around, and Maddock frowned. "Hey, are you alright? You've gone as pale as that wall behind you."

"Yeah, sorry." He put his hand on the metal stand to support himself. "Just remembering the good old times. You know, when one of the brothers distracted the guard so his brother could have a chat. You know, fun days."

"Yeah, well, if those two clowns are still living, I'll give you the gun so you can shoot them yourself. If your crazy plan works, that is." Maddock spun him around. "That's your cue to prove your worth."

Blakey nodded. He turned to face the wall then began to run his fingers over the surface. From where he stood, Maddock saw all the cracks criss-crossing the wall; it reminded him of some ancient mosaic. "I wonder what's behind that wall?"

"We'll soon find out," murmured his cellmate. "Be prepared to witness some Blakey magic." He placed the hammer against the wall at head height and gave Maddock an almost normal grin before he smashed the head of the hammer against the concrete.

Maddock saw two things. First of all, the impact achieved a result. A piece of concrete the size of his foot dropped onto the floor. Second, Maddock believed he finally saw another side of Blakey. The expression that he pulled when that hammer smashed into the wall could only be described as bestial.

"There you go, what did I tell you?" He jumped to the left and hit the wall again. "Stress points, you see? One more whack ought to do it." Blakey held the hammer with both hands. He screamed then swung the hammer against the weakened concrete, laughing like a madman when the entire section collapsed like a house of cards. "You gonna stand there gawking, Maddock? I thought you wanted to rescue Stix." Blakey climbed over the rubble. "Well, look at this? Who'd a thought that the laundry was right behind this wall. Shame it wasn't the staff canteen. I'm starving."

Maddock followed him through. He pushed past his cellmate and ran over to the door. Unlike his cellmate, he didn't intend to blunder about the place just hoping they'd stumble over Stix without getting their heads blown off. He tried the door out of habit knowing it should be locked. The door swung open to reveal an empty corridor. "That's not possible," he muttered. What made the situation even more surreal was from where he stood, Maddock could clearly see the door which led to the staircases was open as well.

"You're sure doing a lot of gawking, Maddock. What is it with you and the standing about with your gob open? You look like a deranged goldfish." Blakey squeezed past him. "Unglue your feet from the floor and come on before The Beast throws our mate to the sea dragon?"

Maddock shook away this unexpected turn of events and raced down the corridor. "Oh, shit," he muttered. The reason why the door at this end hadn't shut was due to another guard's corpse slumped against it. Blakey was already there furiously rummaging through the dean man's pockets. The term grave robber sprung to mind. "What are you doing, man? Get up. Like you said, time's wasting."

"The bastard's unarmed!" he cried. "That's so not fair."

Maddock pulled him up by the scruff of the neck. "Leave it, we'll find you one later. Let's find Stix!"

Blakey shrugged him off and gave him a glare that could curdle milk. Just for that moment, Maddock began to wonder if coming back for Blakey was the best idea he'd ever had.

"Yeah, sorry. I guess that..." the little man sighed. "No, it doesn't matter." He nodded over to the stairs. My bet is that he and his pals will head towards the jetty. After all, it is the only way off this place."

"Sounds logical. After you."

Maddock made sure the safety was off before he followed Blakey down the metal steps. At each level, he tried the doors, and wasn't shocked to find that every door he tried refused to budge. Two levels later, they reached the ground level. There were another two levels below this one, but the stairs leading to them were submerged. He dipped his toe in the water and wriggled it about.

"What the hell are you doing?"

"Nothing, just testing out a theory."

"You're so weird sometimes." Blakey slammed his body against the doors and laughed when they opened. "Told you, Maddock. What did I say? I'm your lucky mascot. Bet you're so glad you didn't drop me off the edge now!"

Maddock took his gun out and walked through the doors. As he expected, he saw nobody about apart from Blakey who was dancing about like a clown on speed. "Will you come over here, you idiot?" He saw two large boats tied up. His heart sank. Maddock hoped they'd be bigger - at least larger than Blakey's sea dragon. Neither of them would stand much of a chance against the monster if it decided to attack the boat. Unless they could outrun it. Unless they could figure out some way of using both boats with the empty one as a decoy.

"Look at the size of that boat, Maddock. I bet we could get all the way to Jamaica on that baby!"

"Put the gun down, boy!" thundered a familiar voice.

Maddock's guts rolled when he saw The Beast and one of the Maynard brothers rising from behind three oil drums a few feet from the boat. He saw more shadows moving as heads and shoulders appeared from inside the machine. At least three of them were armed.

Maddock grinned. He shook his head, frustrated that he hadn't listened to his inner voices. "I thought I could smell something bad. Should have guessed it was you." He raised the arm and aimed at The Beast. "Tell your men to put down their guns or you die."

"They'll drop you before you have chance to fire. Now listen to me, boy. I'm only giving you this one chance."

Blakey sidled up to him and leaned close. Maddock squeezed the trigger just as his cellmate violently pushed his arm. The shot missed The Beast and slammed into the man beside him. Before Maddock could fire off another shot, he felt cold metal digging into his side.

"Oh, looks like that guard did have a gun on him. Bad Blakey, I lied again."

CHAPTER SEVEN

The single shot had roused The Prowler from his slumber some time ago. From the conversations he'd overheard after, he guessed that their final guests had arrived. That pleased him so much. Being cooped up inside this metal box hadn't done his muscles any good.

His talents had suffered due to the two years spent in prison. Apart from crawling under their bunk, there hadn't been too many places in here to practice. Even the bunk became to no go area once the guards worked out why he was doing it.

The Prowler was certain to ache once he left this most excellent hiding place, but he saw it as a small price to pay for regaining his freedom. Besides, all talented people were supposed to suffer for their art. He'd read that in a book somewhere. The question of leaving his box had seriously started to rule his thoughts now.

By his estimations, they'd been at sea now for two hours. He hadn't heard voices for one of them so he was going to go out on a limb and say that most of them were amusing in whatever sick and depraved ways they saw fit. As there were no women on board, that meant drinking and gambling. Hopefully, mainly drinking. The more drunk they were, the better he'd feel.

He lifted the lid a crack. The light had dimmed somewhat, so he guessed that night had fallen. He saw no obvious shadow activity, and his senses told him that none of the other inmates were in here with him.

The Prowler trusted his senses intimately. They had never let him down. It was time to do the thing that he was born to do - prowling. On this occasion, they were no valuables to take, nor was there any chance of leaving until they landed. It didn't mean he should not investigate. Besides, his stomach had begun to ask for sustenance a bit back.

Before his courage vanished, he opened the lid wider and poured his body onto the floor, then silently closed the lid before running towards the darkest part of the hold. He waited there, stretching the best he could while listening to the waves. The Prowler smiled to himself. His new friend was close by, following the boat, waiting for the time to open this vessel up like a tin can.

The other beast, the fat inmate who once ruled their prison with a fist of iron was no idiot. He knew the creature would follow them. That's exactly why he brought that captured guard and the prisoners whom he believed were not loyal. The Prowler knew for a fact that if was caught, he too would end up as sea monster bait. This is one of the reasons why he'd been so reluctant to leave his box.

If he was the courageous person who possessed elephant balls, he might have even considered attempting to free the ones in the lock up and help them take over the ship. He had come to terms with who he was many years ago. He felt for the others currently locked up in the cells in the next cabin. He wouldn't be human otherwise. On this occasion, they needed to stay where they were, out of his way. The Prowler had no wish to literally rock the boat.

There were three locked up and another four somewhere else. From what little noise he could make out, two of them were in a cabin above this one. On occasion, The Prowler caught a snatch of high pitched laughter. He guessed that would be that no good little toad, Blakey. He had never liked that one. He was one twisted individual. The Prowler had watched him often, sneaking about, carrying messages from The Beast to the guards in his pocket. Yet, despite this, the little man was not protected. The others regularly beat the crap out of him. The Prowler had reached the disturbing conclusion that Blakey actually enjoyed it.

It wouldn't be The Beast with Blakey; the little man might find the prospect of receiving pain enjoyable, but even he wouldn't act like an excitable monkey in the presence of his boss. This probably meant he was with one of The Beast's henchmen.

The Prowler left the comfort of the shadows and staked out the dark cabin, looking for anything which could prove useful. The eyes settled upon a small hammer left on top of an overturned metal barrel. He grinned to himself. That was just perfect. Deadly in the right hands and yet small enough to easily conceal.

The Prowler noticed a small knife lying on the floor. He turned it around in his fingers then gave the blade a tentative sniff. Apple juice. It would come in handy. He hid this down his sock. There was nothing else of interest here, so he made his way towards the closed door, hoping that those idiots had not had the fortitude to lock it after they had left. He stopped near the single window beside the door and counted to three before taking a swift look outside.

The brief view gave him some more additional information. It wasn't yet dark. The sun was setting to port side of the boat, it's fiery edges touching the water's surface. This was good. The Prowler preferred the dark; it gave him the advantage as he had excellent night vision. His field of vision had showed him no other people, just an empty deck, meaning he could take another look knowing his face wouldn't be seen.

The Prowler did just that. This time, he opened the window a crack and listened. His finely attuned sense of hearing picked out the low murmur of his fellow incarcerated prisoners, and Blakey's really annoying laughter, as well bootsteps. It was the latter which interested him. They would belong to the prisoner who'd been given watch duty. He was the one who might spot The Prowler as he explored this boat.

This made him a threat.

The bootsteps came to a sudden halt and Blakey's laughter stopped before the little man's joviality turned into a short yelp of pain. The Prowler grinned, his imagination had already drawn a rough sketch; he needed to investigate this. He wanted to transform his sketch into a painted picture, especially if they were using blood as red paint as he suspected. Blakey's blood to be exact.

He pushed the hammer into the back of his trousers, hurried over to the door, and eased it open. The only individual who wasn't accounted for was The Beast. His past observations had shown that the big fat man wasn't exactly the type to move about much, preferring his many minions to do his heavy lifting. The chances of The Beast laying in wait outside this cabin all ready to leap on The Prowler once he left here was practically zero.

Even so, this didn't stop him from removing the hammer from his back pocket. As zero chance was still a chance. He heard no bubbly wet breathing, nor could he smell the big fat man's rancid breath. He grinned to himself before replacing the hammer. The Prowler knew exactly where the main facilitator of this little escapade would be residing. He'd be lying about in the boat's comfiest cabin, on top of the ill-gotten gains that he'd taken from the prison and this boat. The Beast was just like the mythical dragon jealously guarding his hoard from all potential thieves.

"Only sweatier and with considerably more pink flesh," he whispered.

The Prowler left the cabin, flattened his body against the wall, and silently closed the door. Four feet of polished wood separated him from the rolling ocean and his new friend. He so ached to disregard his instinctive demeanour of staying hidden in the shadows and rush over to that railing to see if he could spot that majestic animal. It then occurred to him that, apart from stretching his limbs, gaining another sight of his new friend was really the only reason why he left the cabin. He certainly didn't need to invite danger by leaving; he just needed to stretch his legs.

This new personality facet intrigued him, but it didn't surprise The Prowler at all, for he knew that as soon as he set eyes upon the animal, he knew he'd fallen in love. He jerked his head to the side when the ear cringing sound of Blakey's voice reached him. His snivelling, subversive tone was back and in full force, meaning the little man hadn't just been beaten to a pulp after all. So, he wouldn't be privileged in witnessing a beating, although annoying, it wasn't the end of the world. Still, this still needed investigating as The Prowler had to ascertain their exact location before it was safe to search for his new friend.

He ran from the cabin towards the metal steps which would lead him up onto the next level where the crew quarters were. The Prowler knew his way around this craft as he'd already thoroughly explored it before The Beast and his collection of thugs appeared on the scene. He hadn't explored the smaller boat as he knew the fat slime ball would only choose this one; it was how The Beast thought.

There were four more cabins on the deck above him, as well as the bridge. The Beast had declared that as strictly off-limits after the slime ball had programmed in their destination, wherever that was. The Prowler guessed that The Beast had another vessel waiting for them. It made sense considering how far they were from land.

This left him with a choice of four cabins to check. The Beast had the captain's cabin on the top deck so The Prowler didn't need to worry about finding him in one and as none of the remaining three prisoners were not making much effort in concealing themselves, the search should take seconds.

Lights were burning in just one cabin, furthest from the stairs. "They're not even making this challenging," he grunted. Were they not aware that they'd just broken out of a maximum-security prison, and by now half the world's police would be searching for them. In fact, why wasn't the night sky full of helicopters? Surely, this boat should have a tracking beacon installed. The Prowler decided not to pursue that avenue of thinking. It wouldn't be healthy for his brain juice.

He silently made his way up the metal steps while keeping his eyes fixed on that cabin door. This part was dangerous. There would be nowhere to run if any of them opened that door. The Prowler trusted his luck and raced across the deck. As soon as he reached the first cabin, he took position behind it and kindly asked his heart to slow down. This took some time as the 'nowhere to go' part of his situation continued to resonate around the inside of his skull, almost to the stage where he almost ran back and crawled back inside his box.

"You have balls," he whispered. Granted, they weren't the size of an elephant, but nevertheless, The Prowler did possess a pair. He also had a hammer. There would be no going back until he acquired more information. "You've already wasted enough time."

He moved away from the wall and sneaked past the remaining cabins. As he neared his destination, the stink of beer and tobacco smoke assaulted his nose. They must be having a right old time in there. Finally, he passed the closed door and the open window before ducking round the back. The Prowler sank to the floor, feeling like he'd just run a marathon.

"Sure, he told me where we were going."

The sudden noise startled him so much, he almost banged the back of his head against the wall. It sounded like he was in the room with them. That was the remaining Maynard brother. He'd recognise that Bronx accent anywhere.

"So, come on then, spill the beans. Don't leave us in suspense."

It took him a moment to place that voice. The Prowler finally nailed it though. That belonged to Devon Palmer - some greasy shit who followed The Beast around like a bad smell. Dare he look through the window? The light out here was now almost non-existent, so as long as he didn't press his face against the glass, nobody in there would see him. He crawled away from the wall before kneeling up. Yeah, they were, all three of them. What a sad collection of human rejects.

Blakey and Palmer sat opposite each other. They'd found a deck of cards. Palmer had a can of lager and a lit cigar beside him, whereas Blakey didn't. A quick dart towards the door explained why.

Palmer held a can of lager in one hand whilst his other dirty paw contained a half-smoked cigar. It wasn't too difficult to reconstruct Palmer's entrance. He crawled back to the wall to continue his information gathering.

"Seriously, that's what the boss told me."

"Wait, you're telling me there's a floating holiday in the middle of the Atlantic?" Palmer laughed. "He's telling you big porkies, mate."

"Yeah, even I couldn't come out with a lie that bad."

The hair on the back of The Prowler's neck stood up. Why did the sound of Blakey's voice make him want to punch the little man into the middle of next week?

"One more word out of you, dogshit, and you're going in the cage with your pals. Listen to me, Palmer. It is true. Come on, where else do you think we're going? I mean, this thing ain't gonna get us to Mexico now is it?"

Could Maynard's claim be true? It certainly wasn't beyond the realms of reality. None of the prisoners had access to the outside world. They were essentially cut off. Hell, he didn't even know who had become the next US president. Sure, the guard knew but they were also aware that if they shared any information, no matter how trivial, they could find themselves sharing cells with the prisoners.

"The boss told me that the place is a Mecca for the filthy rich.

It's teaming with classy girls, enough money to buy your own country, and to make the deal even sweeter, it's in international waters, meaning the law can't touch us. I'm telling you, Palmer. It's perfect."

"Look, I'll believe when I see it."

The Prowler listened to the conversation for a little longer. They'd all reached the point of bragging about what they were going to do once they reached the resort. He couldn't care less for their manly boasting and decided to return to his box. This new development did give him some hope. This meant that it should be easier for him to slip away and lose himself. It wouldn't be too difficult to obtain passage to another port where he could start a new life, knowing that he would finally be free. The Prowler might even postpone that dream if this resort turned out to be as profitable as those idiots were suggesting.

"Me? Oh, I want to get myself a spear-gun."

The Prowler's ears pricked up, wondering why Maynard would want such a weapon on a holiday resort.

"There's bound to be a few lying about. You know for killing sharks and really big fish. Those rich folks love doing stuff like that. Me and my brother had one when we were kids. They're great."

"I thought you live in the middle of the country? You know, on dry land and all that."

"True, Palmer, all too true. Granted, they were no sharks, but there were loads of cats." Maynard chuckled. "At least there were before Toby got the spear-gun."

A cold fury settled in the pit of his stomach. The Prowler listened to the man's words growing mad and madder at each boastful remark.

"Toby went for the head all the time. Me, I went for their backs. I tell you, there's nothing more hilarious than listening to a little pussy cat howl in shock and agony with a metal spike through its back legs."

"You had better get back on watch, you sick bastard," laughed Palmer. "If the boss catches you in here, it's gonna be you with a metal spike in your leg."

The cabin door swung open. The Prowler stayed in the shadows and watched Maynard leisurely walked over to the metal stairs. He whistled a tuneless song and shone his flashlight around the edge of the boat. He waited until the man was descending the stairs before he followed at a discreet distance.

The Prowler took out the hammer. It was a good size and comfortable to hold. The handle wouldn't slip from his tight grip. He looked over the railings and saw the man walking towards the next set of metal steps which led to the holding cells. He was probably going to give the men in that cage some grief.

He couldn't allow that to happen. The Prowler need Maynard pretty much where he was now. Stairs would prove problematic. He ran down the metal stairs, confident that Maynard wouldn't hear him. They didn't call him The Prowler for nothing. He ran over to the whistling man who heard his approach, but was too late to stop the his hammer from smashing into the side of Maynard's head.

He crashed onto the deck, out cold. The Prowler dropped to his knees and frantically checked his pulse. Maynard couldn't die here, this wasn't the time, and it certainly wasn't the place. There was one, but it was faint. That would suit him just fine. Maynard was strong, He'd soon recover. The Prowler quickly retrieved the dropped flashlight and switched it off before throwing that overboard.

The hammer had only initiated his plan. To complete it, he needed another piece of equipment. Thankfully, due to the location where he hit Maynard, it didn't take him long to drag the animal abuser over to it.

The sound of the cabin door opening again froze him to the spot. He was in plain view of anyone who left! He slowly turned to face the door and watched Blakey wobble out of the door. The little man turned and waved. Instinctively, The Prowler waved back. The man was as drunk as a skunk. Could any man become that drunk on a single can of lager, or had that lying toad and Palmer had something else, just waiting for Maynard to leave them alone? He mentally shrugged. Did it really matter?

The little man shuffled down to the next cabin, fell against the door which swung opened, and spilled his body inside. A quiet moan escaping from Maynard brought him back to his current task. There's no way that he could allow this one to start making a fuss. Not yet anyway; not until he had finished.

The Prowler grabbed the thick metal chain which hung down beside him. He sat the unconscious man up and fastened it under Maynard's arms. He followed the chain up to the top of the crane then down the thick steel arm, all the way down to the connecting wheel beside him. There was just one more thing he need to do before continuing. The Prowler slipped out the vegetable knife, opened the man's shirt and cut a thin line down his chest.

"Time to dance," he snarled.

The Prowler used the wheel to lift him into the air before manually swinging Maynard across the deck, past the railing and over the side of the boat. The man hung there like a joint of meat while his life fluid dripped into the water.

"Come on, my friend. This is my gift to you."

Maynard's eyes suddenly snapped open. It took him a moment to focus before he started to struggle. "Hey, what the?" He blinked rapidly. "You, what's going on, this isn't funny, Tell the boss that I..."

His words dried up at the sight of a shadow below him as large as the boat.

"Oh, God, please. No, don't do this!"

"Nothing more hilarious than listening to them howl in shock and agony." The Prowler stepped away from the railing as the leviathan rose out of the ocean and snapped his huge jaws over the shrieking man, cutting him in half. "I said that I would look after you, my friend." He placed the hammer beside the crane then hurried away from the scene. He knew where the hammer had originated from; he also knew what the two Maynard brothers used to do to Blakey every week.

Several lights came on just as The Prowler entered the cabin. The shouting started at the same time as he closed the lid on his box.

CHAPTER EIGHT

That sudden inrush of water missed her toes by inches. What the hell was she playing at? Even now, after everything that had happened to her, Georgia was still taking stupid risks. She took a single step backwards and watched the black water fill in the imprint of her feet that she'd left in the wet sand. She'd been lucky that time.

Just how long had she been out here? It felt like a few minutes but there's no way that could be right. It had been daylight when she'd run out of the guest entrance sobbing and screaming for help that obviously wasn't there.

She wiped her palm down her face while keeping a close eye on that encroaching wave. They were close by and using the darkness as perfect cover. Oh, yeah, the little bastards were out there. Silent, invisible, and deadly. Just as dangerous as their other unwanted guests.

Georgia slowly backed away, resisting the urge to spin around and run back to the buildings. No, she daren't do that. Those dark monolithic structures were far more dangerous at night. There were too many corners and hiding places for those vile little animals. Her feet soon hit the gravel which marked the boundary of the resort's golden shore.

When Georgia first arrived here, she'd been utterly blown away by the view. The designers and landscape artists had done an incredible job in creating the perfect paradise island facsimile. Everything looked the part, even down to the coconut trees a few metres to her left. The only thing that the designers couldn't totally hide was the transparent barrier around the floating island. Not that anyone really noticed, and you couldn't see it once the sun went down.

"It is a miracle of modern technology," she muttered, remembering the quote the resort owners placed on the front of their promotional brochures. As far as she was concerned, the bastards needed to go back to the drawing board. To stop everything but water from entering the island, they had installed a carbon fibre mesh between the barrier and the island plate. It hadn't stopped those little black nightmares, though. The octopuses had simply crawled up the barrier and flopped over the edge.

The water would continue to advance up the beach until it reached the gravel before beginning its slow journey back towards the barrier. She intended to stay here at this exact spot until the sun came up. By that time, she hoped that the retreating tide had stranded all those octopuses on the beach. Georgia wanted to watch them all gasp their last few breaths before the seagulls landed and feasted on their drying flesh. The plan had appeal, considering she had nowhere else to go now.

Watching those things flounder in the sand wouldn't bring the ones she'd lost back to life, but Georgia firmly believed that it would help, in some way, to help recover the emotions which bled from her body before fleeing here.

She felt dead inside, like someone had scraped out her insides.

Why could she not remember the last few hours? Georgia clearly recalled everything from the moment that monster took her Liam, all the way up to finding herself at that barrier, smashing her fists against the translucent material and screaming for help. She even remembered that poor boy up in the observation gallery pleading for anyone to try and save him.

She couldn't be the only person at the resort to survive through the past few hours. There were almost eighty guests and another eighty members of staff here to look after them. They couldn't all be dead. That was impossible. The water had flooded most of the lower levels, but the floors above would have been just fine. Georgia knew for a fact that the Island Spot restaurant near the guest entrance was always busy. The people in there eating when the disaster happened could have easily escaped.

Meaning, there had to be other people somewhere close by. She gazed across the dark beach, desperately listening for sounds of other people. If they were out here. Nobody were making their presence known.

"Hello!" she shouted. "Is there anybody here!" Georgia heard noises but they sure weren't human. Two small shadows flopped and rolled across the sand. "Shit." She scurried backwards until her back smacked against a metal chair. "You'll do," she snarled, picking it up. Georgia stood her ground as two black octopuses approached her. She waited until the vile things were about to jump before lifting the chair over her head and smashing it down. Two satisfying wet splats silenced them forever.

That explained why she could only hear the waves hitting the barrier.

She pulled the chair off the corpses, groaning in disgust at the slimy mess which dripped off the chair legs. It wasn't much of a weapon, but it did the job. Georgia stopped walking and listened. She couldn't see anything else, but they those little nightmares were out there as she had just proved. Killing two wouldn't make a dent in their numbers. From what she had seen while running through the buildings, there could be thousands of the little bastards out there.

It might not be such a good idea to stay up here after all. If she just so happened to close her eyes and fall asleep she might never wake up and the despicable thought of those creatures eating her alive made Georgia want to physically vomit.

The very fact that she hadn't succumb to those things shocked the hell out of her considering that she still couldn't remember anything after reaching that barrier all the way up to a few minutes ago.

Her last memory was of staring in disbelief at the scene just beyond the island. She knew why the Liopleurodon had a raging appetite. She'd been eating for three. It also explained why she had turned the sea into a killing zone. She had given birth. Her two babies. Dolphin-sized replicas of their mother raced through the lumpy crimson soup, hoovering up anything that wasn't water.

It suddenly seemed incredibly important to retrieve her lost memories. She took a deep breath, swallowed her fear, and attempted to bring herself to go back and live through the moments after the Liopleurodon had snatched her Liam out of her hands.

The suddenness of the attack literally took her breath away. Georgia wanted to drop to her knees and wail like a banshee, yet her own instinct for self-preservation pushed her back, away from the hatch. It was only a few feet, but that small distance saved her from joining Liam.

The huge animal launched its body through that hole, its gigantic head darted towards her, and she heard herself shrieking when those jaws opened wide and snapped at the air just inches from her body. Georgia managed to scramble up a set of metal steps, bolted to the far wall before the beast could return. The chances of it managing to pull the rest of its body through that small hole were next to impossible, but in her panicking mind a thick haze of terror had covered up such adherences to basic fact.

Georgia wrenched open the door at the top of the steps and ran through it, finding herself inside another area of the resort she'd never known about. Judging from the amount of dust covering the floor, she guessed that nobody had been in here for quite some time. Not that she cared. She turned around and watched the monster slowly slide back under the water. "Ambush predator," she said before bursting into tears. She slammed the door shut and held onto the handle, knowing that if her hands let go, she'd end up falling against it, sliding to the ground, and staying there until she gave up on life.

When the sound of tearing metal reached her she ran whimpering down the neglected corridor, heading for the next door. She burst through and stopped dead. Georgia walked forward a couple of paces, totally shocked at where she'd ended up. The door behind her swung back and clicked shut. This was just unreal. Georgia had found herself inside one of the more exclusive clothing boutiques in the resort.

She turned around and saw that her exit was now a full-length mirror. Georgia stood in front of it while her drenched reflection stared back at her. That woman wasn't her; it couldn't be. Her reflection looked like she'd just stepped out of a horror movie. Georgia lifted her arms and saw, for the first time, that her sleeves were drenched in Liam's blood.

Georgia ran from the dressing room. It took her seconds to remove the offending item and find a dry top to slip on. There wasn't anyone in the shop. She wandered towards the front entrance while seeking out any other people. Georgia saw plenty of evidence that something weird had happened in here. The piles of dropped clothing told her that much.

The clothes scattered across the dark red carpet wasn't all that she found unusual. The sunlight streaming through the boutique's decorative glass ceiling bounced off over a dozen patches of what looked like oil stains. Georgia approached the closest one, crouched beside it, and poked the tip of a pencil in the middle. The black stuff wasn't oil; it was way too thick. It reminded her of thick treacle.

"That is totally gross." She left the pencil floating in the mess, stood up, and hurried over to the front doors. Before leaving the boutique, Georgia walked along the glass front and peered down each aisle. There was plenty more clothing, everything from underwear to shirts on the floor, but no sign of another soul.

She headed back to the front doors, slowing down when something else caught her eyes. On the other side of the doors, the carpet was sodden through. Georgia approached the stain and moaned softly when she realised that it wasn't water. That was blood, and by the looks of it, a good few pints. She shivered to herself and rushed out of the shop, suddenly eager to be somewhere else.

Georgia stood outside the boutique and wrapped her arms tight around her chest and looked up and down the resort's main shopping street. They had modelled the entire shopping centre on some fictional stylised 19th century English town, complete with street lamps, working red telephone boxes, and even a couple of post boxes situated at the street's two ends. It was all very quaint, and a little too quaint for her liking. Plus, nearly every shop here was way above her pay grade.

The rich tourists lapped up the olde worlde falseness and spent an absolute fortune in almost every shop.

She pushed her hands into her new jacket then noticed the price tag hanging off her sleeves. It didn't surprise her find out that this single item of clothing cost more than two-months wages. She tore the label off and threw it in the air, watching it float down and land on a wooden bench next to another shiny black stain. They were really beginning to freak her out; probably more than the absence of the people.

Where the hell were they? Georgia ran from one shop window to the next and peered through each glass in her attempt to find another human either living or dead - preferably living. Each shop showed her the same picture: dropped items everywhere, from CD's and picture frames, to shoes and watches, but no humans.

There were a few more of those shiny black blobs though.

Georgia reached the last shop on the promenade. Again, the view inside reflected what all the other shops showed her. This time, she stayed put. Not only because there was nowhere else to go, but because this place held so many happy memories.

During her induction, their human resources team adjudicator had brought them all to the Britannia Cafe for their first ever resort lunch. Just like the rest of the shops, it was styled on another English tradition. Unlike all the other tourist traps along the promenade, the prices were more in line with what she could afford. Her father had come from Manchester in the north of the country and ensured the young Georgia knew about her roots. Consequently, she felt right at home sitting in the hard-curved plastic seats while eating steak pie, mash, and mushy peas. Judging from the scarcity of tourists, she wondered if the place was a little too authentic for their tastes.

Looking through the window, Georgia saw plates of food on the tables, a few handbags - even a cell phone lying next to a glass of milk. She should have ignored the scene and left the promenade to continue her search. The natural light streaming through all the transparent ceilings wouldn't light her way indefinitely.

Georgia pushed the door open, entered the cafe, and leaned over the glass counter. It didn't surprise her to discover nobody about. She took a couple of candy bars from the wire display stand next to her then walked over to the end table. She sat down and carefully unwrapped the first candy bar. Before she bit into it, Georgia pushed her forefinger into the cup in front of her. It was still warm.

"I was going to bring you here, Liam," she whispered. It wouldn't have been on their first date. Georgia intended for them to get to know each other a little better before divulging the location of this little hidden gem. Hell, he might already know about it. The place was pretty popular with some of the other staff members who sometimes became bored of the food in the two staff restaurants. "Come on, Georgia, stop it with the pity party, and get your mind working again." Easier said than done. She stood up and bit into the candy bar while walking back over to the counter. It did feel odd being in here without the music the chinking of cutlery and numerous low conversations she used to listen to.

She suddenly froze when it struck her exactly why there were no people about. They'd been evacuated. Of course, they had. As soon as the staff became aware that something had seriously gone wrong, their first job was to ensure the safety of the guests. Each shop worker became responsible for the people in their shop, and it was their duty to take them to one of the three emergency locations situated around the island. They were all on the surface, next to one of the island's dropping off points. Why hadn't any of this clicked until now? They were all trained in the evacuation procedure; it was one of the first things that the team adjudicator showed them.

Georgia ran to the front the shop still unable to believe that she'd been stupid enough not to see the obvious. They must have set off the fire alarms from every shop; they'd have streamed out, filling this promenade, while the workers formed them all into orderly queues, and escorted them to their designated places.

The closest one wasn't far from here, about five-minutes-walk. She'd be there in three, maybe less. Georgia ran out of the resort's shopping district and through one of the residential blocks. This was where the cheaper apartments were located, where holiday makers who won competitions were placed, away from the more luxurious areas further down. Everybody up here should still be alive. God, Georgia had never needed to find another human more in her life. Just somebody else to hold, to comfort, to share her grief. It made her increase her speed.

The main entrance was now in sight; she'd be there in a matter of seconds.

Just as she passed one of the guest doors, something on the other side slammed against the wood. Georgia screamed out in shock and found herself tripping up over her own feet. The noise came again, only this time it was far softer. Was there anybody in there? She managed to get to her feet and calm her racing heart down before slowly approaching the bright yellow door. She grabbed hold of the handle and eased it down, still expecting it to be locked tight.

The door opened and swung inwards. She saw nothing but bitch black. No lights, no movement; it was like looking into the blackness of outer space. Georgia turned her attention to the bottom of the door and saw a small pool of red fluid leaking out from under the door. It wasn't blood, that much she did know.

"Is there anybody in there?" she shouted, expecting nothing back.

She jumped again when the sound of something heavy crashing onto the floor reached her. That came from the kitchen area. Every room in the cheap apartments shared the same floor plan. Georgia took one step inside and allowed her eyes to adjust to the darkness. Within a few seconds, the blurred shapes of the furniture started to form, and she could make out the door which led into the next room.

Before she went any further, Georgia pulled the door away from the wall and crouched down behind it where she found a plastic bottle still half full. The smell gave it away. Someone had thrown a bottle of fruit cordial across the room. She didn't even bother trying to figure out why; it just meant that she wasn't alone.

She ran over to the door then paused, sure that something in here had moved. Georgia turned around and stared hard at the largest piece of furniture. The shape suggested that it was a sofa. Could it have been a cat? Pets weren't allowed, but on occasion it had been known for a guest to sneak one onto the resort. Whatever it was - if it was anything - she didn't see it.

Georgia turned back and pulled open the door, eager to find out who was inside the apartment. The room beyond wasn't in darkness thanks to a single spluttering candle on the far side standing on a bookcase shelf.

The illumination showed her the carpet full of more of those shiny black pools of slime; unlike the ones in the shopping area, these ones moved. The nearest to her foot unrolled a tentacle and whipped it to the side. She stayed still, not even daring to breathe. An octopus wasn't aggressive to humans, even in such large numbers, but the malevolence she felt rising from these things, no matter how irrational it was, couldn't be ignored. When the nearest octopus rolled its tentacle back inside its body, she slowly turned her head. In the dim light, Georgia saw another three of the things on the furniture.

She wanted to get out of here, to run to that evacuation point as fast as she could, but even Georgia knew that none of these things had thrown that plastic bottle against the door. There were two more doors, each one at either side of that bookcase. She opened her mouth then closed it. Shouting out probably wasn't a good idea. Georgia stepped over two of the animals then slowly tip-toed through the rest of them, while keeping her fingers on the wall. Once her fingertips reached the door-frame, Georgia sighed with relief, then slapped her hand over her mouth when three of the octopuses quivered before darting across the carpet. They weaved through their companions without touching them and launched their bodies out through the open door and vanished into the next room.

Her mind threatened to tilt, when it occurred to her that if she had called out, those would have landed on her front. While she had no idea what species these belonged to, Georgia knew of at least one species: the blue ringed octopus which, if provoked, transmitted a toxin through its bite that could kill a human within a few hours. These things certainly weren't docile or solitary. They were fast as well; she'd never seen one move so fast before.

Georgia's hand crawled up the side of the door while she kept her daze firmly fixed upon the dozens of glistening animals. How could they stay out of water for so long? After what seemed like an age, her fingers finally grasped the door handle. She said a small silent prayer which involved finding lighting in the next room, another human, some kind of weapon, and definitely no more of these horrible wet bastards.

She pushed the handle down, aware that the noise had already attracted some interest. Three of them had begun to stir and throw out their tentacles, waving them through the air like they were tasting it.

Without pausing, Georgia pushed the door open threw herself through the widening gap before slamming her body against the other side, mumbling in terror at the noise of their soft bodies hitting the other side of the door.

"I don't believe it; there's somebody else who's alive!"

A pair of bulging blue eyes set into the face of a terrified twenty-something man stared down at her. He had taken up position crouching on top of a wooden wardrobe next to the bed. Looking around, she saw a dozen or so more candles, as well as a couple of high-powered flashlights rigged to the bedroom ceiling light-fitting, which explained why she could see.

From her position, he didn't look hurt, not unless you counted the many creases in his high quality black suit. She couldn't see any cuts, bruises, or bleeding. He obviously wasn't part of the resort staff. "Hello," she said, smiling. "I'm Georgia. Can you tell me your name?" The young man continued to stare, his gaze darting from her to the door and back again. Those things outside had stopped banging their bodies against the wood.

"I bet there's thousands of them outside now." He climbed down from the cupboard, sat cross-legged in the middle of the bed, and started to rock back and forth. "No, you don't have to answer that. Of course, there are. I mean, where else would they go?" He swallowed hard. "Christ, they're not going to go now are they? Not now you're here. Not now they know there's more food in here for them to dine on." He laughed. "Almost enough to go round."

Georgia stopped smiling when it dawned on her that he wasn't going to be another Liam. This young man was more scared than she was. "What's your name?" she repeated. "I mean, I assume you do have one, right?" He stopped his rocking motion as soon as Georgia moved away from the door. "Is this your place?"

He shook his head. "Christ no. This is like one of those bargain basement shacks where the poor people go. I have an executive suite, about three levels below, right opposite the Marina Joy Casino. Oh, God, what the fuck is going on here?" He stood up. "Wait, you're staff. I recognise the trousers." He jumped off the bed. "So why don't you tell me what the hell is going on here?" He stopped inches from her. "Have you any idea who I am? I could get this place shut down within hours and slap an injunction on everybody who works here so fast, you wouldn't believe. Hell, you lot will be paying back fines from now until you die of old age!"

Georgia smiled sweetly at the man before she violently pushed him. He wheeled backwards until his spine slammed into the wooden bed post. The man growled and jumped back on his feet. He only stopped when Georgia closed her fingers around the door handle. "Now, I want you to calm down, mister. Take a deep breath then tell me your name. We are both in this dire situation together, and you raising your voice and acting like a petulant child will get us nowhere." She paused. "Now, are we calm?"

After a few seconds, he nodded. "Yeah, I guess. I'm Donovan Hughes, and I came here for two weeks of rest, relaxation, and to spend as much of my father's money as I could."

"Very good, now we're getting somewhere." She removed her hand from the door handle. "So, why didn't you leave when they sounded the fire alarm, Donovan?"

He frowned. "There was no fire alarm."

So much for her theory. "Okay, why don't you tell me what happened? Maybe it can help us finding a way out of here."

"I can't see how."

"Please?"

"Okay, if it makes you feel any better. I was on the promenade, enjoyed a pot of tea at that quaint Limey joint. You know it?!"

"Yeah, I do." That was unexpected. She must have sat in his chair, and it must have been his tea she dipped her finger into. From how he described this apartment earlier, she thought that cafe was the last place he'd go into. "Carry on."

"Well, I needed to use the restroom, and would you believe it, some ugly broad got there before me. Anyway, there I was, crossing my legs and generally wanting the broad to hurry up when, all of a sudden, there's this scream." Blood drained from Donovan's face. "It came from opposite the cafe. I jumped up just as this group of young girls ran out the shop next to us. The screams then started to come from every direction. The big fella behind the counter ran over to the door and looked out before turning to the five customers in the shop. He told us all to form an orderly line so he could take us to the evacuation point. Can you believe that? You know, like it was some fire drill in kindergarten. At this moment, the ugly broad burst through the restroom door and let me tell you, there's was no way she was going to join any kind of line."

Donovan pointed to the door behind her. He looked close to fainting.

"She had one of those black slimy things attached to her face.

Oh, God, it was horrible!" He looked straight at Georgia. "It had crawled out of the toilet. Can you imagine that? That could have been me, you know. If I had gone in just before her, I'd be dead, with all those things wrapping their tentacles around my body. See, there wasn't only one, there were loads of them by now, all racing through that open door, and attaching themselves on the woman. I took my eyes off her just for a moment and found the same scenes happening outside on the promenade."

"What did you do?"

"What do you think I did? I'm not an idiot, unlike all those other crazy people. I wasn't going to go out there and end up being attacked. I played it safe and ran into the restroom, slammed down the toilet lid, locked myself in there, and waited until the screaming stopped."

This guy was a real hero. Such an upstanding member of the human race.

"I guess I stayed in there for about ten minutes." He shrugged. "Yeah, that sounds about right. I opened the door a crack and found myself alone. I saw no other people in the cafe. Not even the fat ugly woman. I have no idea where she went."

Georgia didn't either. She couldn't have just vanished into thin air. "I take it there was nobody outside the cafe either?"

He shrugged again. "I didn't bother looking. All I cared about was getting the hell out of Dodge. It's only when I got to the door of this dingy apartment when I saw them all. There were in front of me blocking my exits. I tell you, there had to be thousands of the horrible slimy little bastards, all stopping me from leaving this stupid resort. I'm going to sue this place for every cent when I get out of here."

"Yeah, well. That's not going to happen unless we work together and think of some way to get past all those animals outside this door."

"I've been having a bit of think about that little problem. Thanks to you, I might have figured out a viable option," he said, smiling.

She saw no humour in that expression. Georgia now began to wish that she'd stayed in that cafe for a few more moments and grabbed something to defend herself. "I'm not sure I want to hear this, Donovan."

"Well, it's pretty simple, actually. Those things only went for that woman; they ignored everyone else. Hell, one of them even scarpered across my table in its bid to reach her. From what I remember from looking out of the window, pretty much the same happened on the promenade."

Donovan climbed off the bed. He reached inside the cabinet and pulled out a long knife. Georgia knew exactly what he intended to do. Oh, Christ! The evil bastard was going to sacrifice her so he could live! The grinning man slowly approached her.

"I'm a peaceful man. Believe me, I'd rather me and you were making out on this bed. You're not that bad looking. Not quite up to the standard I'm used to, but beggars can't be choosers. Look, I'll give you a chance. Slide the blade along your wrists. I promise, it's quite painless."

"Are you serious?"

"Of course, I am. Look, I don't wish to be crude but it's only logical. You're a nothing. Some scrappy nobody, working at some low skill job with very little prospects. I'm worth over ninety million dollars and own one of the largest aerospace companies in Europe." He turned the knife so the blade faced upwards. "Admit it, you'll be doing yourself a favour."

Georgia's smile matched the one that Donovan wore. She held out her arms and walked forward. "You're right. Why should I bother continuing to live?" As soon as Georgia was within distance, she kicked him as hard as she could in between his legs. He groaned softly but didn't move, so she booted him again.

Donovan dropped to his knees. She snatched the knife out of his trembling hands.

"I can't believe that people like you still exist!" Georgia pushed the knife down her belt then dragged the weeping man closer to the door.

"No, please!" His slug-like tongue ran over both his lips. "You can't do this."

"I think you'll find that I can." Georgia grabbed the handle and pulled it down before easing the door open.

The first black octopus scuttled through the opening gap and launched itself at the shrieking man's face, wrapping its eight tentacles around the back of his head. Muffling his screams.

Several more ran in and attached their bodies around Donovan's limbs. The trickle then became a deluge as all the slimy things from the next room flooded in.

She leapt over his shuddering body and ran through the dark rooms and out into the mail hallway. Georgia then hurried away, daring herself not to look back. Before walking out into the bright sunshine, she paused by the main entrance. A side door behind a customer service desk was wide open. Georgia backtracked and peered inside. Just like the clothing shop, there were a few pieces of garments scattered around the tiled floor. The scene didn't seem all that strange until she saw a collection of teeth lying on top of a grey sock. Everything about her recent exploits suddenly slotted into place.

An octopus like other cephalopods feed by injecting their food with a toxic digestive juice which basically liquidised their food's internal organs. They drank their victims like cold, lumpy soup. What if this species possessed the ability to dissolve bones as well?

She pushed the sock with her foot and watched three of the loose teeth roll under some metal shelving. It sounded impossible, but since when did anything today made any sense? It would explain why they only target a single victim. There was too much material for one octopus to liquefy but this wouldn't be an issue if thirty attacked.

Georgia brought herself back to the present. Her hands reached behind her and found the knife. She had totally forgotten about that. The blade glinted in the moonlight. That edge did look as keen as Donovan suggested. By the looks of the rough scratches along the two edges, she suspected that the man had put some work into making it sharper.

Well, it wasn't exactly a rocket launcher, but she'd be able to chop off a few limbs if any of them got too close.

Her thoughts of waiting until the sun came up suddenly left her when the resort's emergency generator kicked in, and all the lights came back on.

That generator hadn't come on by itself, meaning somebody in the building had turned it on. She grinned to herself and walked back to the entrance doors. She knew exactly what to do now. The resort had two weapons stores located close to the main command section.

She was going to find a big enough gun and blow that Liopleurodon to kingdom come.

CHAPTER NINE

Where the knife had come from didn't really matter, not in the great scheme of things anyway. Sure, he did give it some thought, but apart from the ones he'd seen and the guys in here, Maddock had no clue as to who else was aboard. A secret associate, perhaps? He did consider that it might be a plant, some paper-thin excuse to shoot him in the head, but these clowns didn't need a reason. Besides, most of them only had about a dozen brain cells rattling around in their thick skulls.

It hadn't been his old pal Blakey, that's as sure as mustard. If that slimy worm had a knife, he wasn't going to give it to Maddock, not after what he'd done, the dirty little weasel. Not that it had helped him much. Maddock had watched with interest as two of The Beast's cronies dragged the whimpering idiot down those stairs feet first.

They made sure that Blakey's head cracked against each step. Bang, bang, bang, it went all the way down to the bottom.

He almost felt sorry for the little man.

Almost.

Two hours had gone by since those goons had brought the squealing rat down here. Two hours since his cosy little group had acquired their new addition. Thankfully, at least for Blakey, the goons had thrown him into a separate cell. Probably a good thing, too, as it would have been such a waste to lose his new find on Blakey.

There it was, right beside him, just inside the bars, covered by a green shirt which hadn't been there when he'd fallen asleep. If it hadn't been for the sound of the back of Blakey's thick head bouncing off those steps, he might not have noticed it until it was too late. Wouldn't that have been absolutely hilarious?

Maddock got to his feet. He glanced at his two companions. Stix maintained his dopey look. He knew better than to take his blank expression for granted. Behind those bright blue eyes, the man was ready to fight. He'd give their new guards a fight. Not that any of them would be stupid enough to try anything on with Stix. The guy might only be just over five foot, but he was built like a bulldozer.

The guy in the corner was an unknown. Maddock had no idea how he would react when they came for them. The guard was a newbie; he'd only been transferred from some European jail a couple of weeks ago. Hell, they didn't even know his real name.

They'd get their chance to watch the guard soon; that too was as sure as mustard. The boat reached their destination a few minutes ago. Maddock resisted the urge to check that his knife was still there as he didn't want any of the others to know he had it, especially Blakey. That worm was bound to open his gob and grass as soon as that door opened.

"Where do you think we are?"

Maddock shrugged. He couldn't answer Stix's question.

"We're at a holiday resort called Echo-Babylon."

He glanced down at the guard. "Oh, so you do speak." Maddock walked past Stix and crouched down facing him. "Care to elaborate?"

"He ain't gonna say shit to you, Maddock!" cried Blakey. "He just waiting and hoping the others are too busy with you so he can escape."

"Why don't you shut your mouth."

"Oh, and you're gonna make me, Stix?"

The thick set man wrapped his fingers around the metal bars. "Yes. I'm going to make you, Blakey. Just you wait."

Before Maddock could tell them both to shut up, the door at the top of the stairs opened wide. Two of The Beast's men sauntered down, and both were armed. The grins plastered over their ugly mugs spoke volumes. They were here to end them. He wasn't the only one who'd reached that assessment either. Blakey had upturned his bunk and was cowering behind the base while weeping.

"Can I help you two gentlemen?" Maddock joined Stix at the bars. "How about a drink? I have a bottle of single malt in here. Just open this door, and I'll be more than happy to share."

"Oh, ain't you a comedian!" laughed Palmer. He raised his gun. "Let's see you laugh after I've put a bullet in your face."

Before he had time to fire, Stix reached into his pocket, pulled out something shiny and red, and then threw at straight at Palmer. It was a balloon. Maddock had no idea where he'd found that, but he did know that it wasn't full of water.

"You dirty bastard!" he spluttered, while wiping cold piss off his face. "I'm so going to kill you for that. I'm going to kill all of you!"

Palmer had unintentionally closed the gap between them by a couple of inches. Maddock couldn't reach him, but the raging man beyond the bars had obviously forgotten about Stix's extraordinary long arms. The man's lightning reactions took Palmer totally off guard when he reached through the thick bars and managed to snatch the gun barrel. The soaking wet man pulled the trigger, Stix dropped to his knees, and let out a quiet gasp.

Palmer staggered back. "Told you!" he shouted, waving his gun about. "Said I'd kill you! Now it's your turn, guard. Hell, I should have done you first."

A lake of thick blood spread out from under his cell mate's slumped body. It passed under the door and dripped into a run off built into the concrete. Maddock knew that Palmer's gun had switched from Stix to the guard and suspected that the unnamed man probably had just seconds to live.

He stepped over the body and walked across to the door while taking out the knife. Palmer had spotted the knife, but it hadn't registered, just like the knife's location hadn't registered until now. Maddock reached the door and gripped the bars with one hand. He waited for Palmer to scream out his last insult before pushing against the bars.

The door clicked open. Maddock dropped to one knee and threw the knife at Palmer's chest. The blade slammed into his heart killing him instantly. He dived forward and managed to grab Palmer's gun and took shelter behind the man's corpse just as the other prisoner let loose. He fired three rounds; one hit the floor and the other two punched into Palmer's body. Maddock kept his head down and fired blind.

Maddock heard the door slamming shut and lifted his head. He guessed the other prisoner wasn't keen on being on the other end of a gun.

"He'll be back, you know. Back with numbers, and then you'll end up like Stix. See if I'm not right."

It didn't take the fool long to start baiting him to try and sow the doubt seeds. Maddock stood up and flipped Blakey the bird.

"Oh yeah, very clever. So mature."

The little man suddenly shut up when Maddock pulled the knife from the corpse. He glared at Blakey while he licked both sides clean. He turned around, ran back into the cell, and checked the man's pulse. The man was dead. "Shit. I'm sorry, dude."

"Are you going to kill me now?"

"What? Of course, I'm not, man. I ain't no murderer. Besides, you saved my life."

"How do you reckon that?"

Maddock helped the man up. "The way I see it, if you hadn't have been in here then Palmer would have shot me as well as Stix."

The guard sighed heavily. "Fair enough. You are aware that I should be doing everything in my power to keep you in this cage while I go find the relevant authorities."

"Yeah, figured as much."

"I'll give you a couple of minutes to lose yourself."

He gave the man a smart salute before leaving the cage and running towards the stairs.

"Hey, what about me? Come on, Maddock. You can't leave me in here. Where do you think the knife came from?"

Maddock stopped. "So that was you?"

"Course it was. Who else would do it? Come on. Let me out. Hey, and I unlocked your cage door."

"What do you think, fella?" he asked the guard. "Could it be him?"

"I think you already know the answer to that, Maddock. Besides, that knife appeared after he was thrown in there."

"You dirty grassing shit!" he snarled. "I hope someone does a number on you. Oh, yeah, someone is gonna plug you real good."

Maddock threw open the door, left the cabin, and ran towards a set of metal ladders bed to the wall hoping it would take him up to the deck. He could still hear Blakey mouthing off to that guard. So, according to the guard, they'd landed at some floating holiday resort? Was he serious? It sounded a little far-fetched to Maddock. Then again, since the fun and games back at the prison, he wasn't sure if anything could surprise him. He grabbed the rungs, climbed to the top, and slowly poked his head through the hatch. Maddock saw more cabins, a polished wooden deck, and no people. He also found that they had indeed docked.

Just beyond the boat, he saw a huge structure build from glass, steel, and red brick. Above the largest doors there was a large banner which read 'WELCOME TO ECHO-BABYLON'.

"We'll, fancy that," he muttered. Maddock climbed up the remaining steps and ran over to the railing, keeping his head down, just in case. The scene which greeted him once he reached the railing made him wonder if he should have stayed inside that cage.

To the west of him, an artificial beach stretched towards the Atlantic Ocean. Only Maddock couldn't see any sign of the water as a solid mass of those vile black animals totally surrounded the resort. A transparent wall separated them from that writhing mass of invertebrates, but it wasn't stopping them from invading the beach. They climbed the barrier with some difficulty, their suckers kept slipping off the surface, and the animals fell back onto the backs of their companions. Even so, with every ten which failed to gain purchase, one of them managed to flop over the top and land on the golden sand.

There must be thousands of them around the perimeter. To make his day well and truly complete, Maddock noticed the unmistakable shape of the nightmarish monster which had caused so much carnage back at the prison. So, it had followed their boat after all.

That's all he needed. Like those octopuses weren't problematic enough. Whilst locked in that cage, Maddock had spent most of his time trying to figure out a viable way get back home and to stay free. He did not want to spend the rest of his life looking over his shoulder. Maddock had decided to stay as far away from his place of birth as he could, and after giving it some considerable thought, he went for one of the countries in the UK that sounded like his best option.

Before the guard announced their destination, he guessed that they'd be meeting up with another ship. Maddock hadn't given it much thought as how he was to get onto that ship without The Beast's men shooting him full of holes. Perhaps this place would supply Maddock with all his needs. It shouldn't be too difficult to lose himself here and secure himself a passage to wherever he wanted to go.

So why did he feel like he had just climbed out of a frying pan and straight into a fire? He shifted his gaze away from those horrible things slipping over that wall and scanned the rest of the beach. He saw no human activity anywhere. Then again, who in their right mind would stick around after finding out that thousands of black octopuses were doing their best to sliver across the sand?

He turned his attention to the large two-storey brick building. Considering this was supposed to be a holiday resort, the place didn't exactly strike him as elaborate. When the guard mentioned their final destination, Maddock imagined half a dozen white hotels reaching for the clouds. Maddock had seen more artistic cowsheds.

"The tip of the iceberg?" That made sense. Most of the resort must be below the surface. There were plenty of windows as well as what looked like an observation level at the end of the building. He saw no sign of life over there either.

Maddock couldn't stay here, that much was certain. It wouldn't take those little black monsters long to sliver their way here. He ran across the deck and carefully made his way over the wooden ramp and onto the jetty.

Why hadn't that monster attacked the boat while they'd been travelling? He shook his head in annoyance. Why was he even asking himself that question? He ought to be thankful that it hadn't, leave it, and focus on the fact that there was nobody to greet him.

He stamped his foot on the wood. It sure felt solid, but it wasn't. This place was about as vulnerable as the place from where he'd just escaped. It might have better accommodation, not as many locks, and nicer people, but it was still a floating platform like the prison. Meaning it was still vulnerable. That thought made him pause again. What if the same disaster that hit the prison happened here, too?

It would explain the lack of resort staff and guests, as well as all those octopuses on the water's edge. Christ, it really was out of the frying pan and into the fire. So where does this leave him? He shrugged.

"I'm not dead yet."

Maddock's boots landed on concrete when he jumped off the jetty. There were a couple of barrels in the corner next to a grey wall, a handcart, and a pile of broken wooden crates near the barrels. They had docked at a service jetty, meaning the visitors must land on another, much larger jetty, probably on the other side of the island. That's where Maddock needed to get to and find a ship made for ocean travel.

Would he be able to get around the other side of the island without going through the building? Maddock wasn't sure that he should chance it considering before too long, this beach would be black with octopus. He couldn't afford to let them trap him.

"Shit," he muttered when he spied one of them climbing up the boat's bow. It wasn't alone either. He ground his teeth in annoyance and ran back onto the boat. Maddock couldn't leave them two in there. Even if Blakey more than deserved it.

The guard was already climbing out of the hold when Maddock jumped onto the deck.

"I thought I told you to vanish, Maddock."

"We have bigger problems." He ran over to the man. "Look over there."

The guard stared at the approaching animals for a few seconds before looking back at Maddock. "Stowaways from the prison?"

Maddock stepped back and allowed the man to climb onto the deck. "You'd better see for yourself." He jumped onto the steps. "While you're having your mental seizure, I'll see if I can get Blakey out." He hurried down the steps and pushed through the door into the hold. Blakey saw him but didn't say anything. The little man was too busy sitting in the corner of his cell with his arms wrapped around his legs. Maddock ran over to Palmer and patted him down. He found the key in the dead man's back pocket along with a wallet. He kept hold of that and ran over to the bars. The man still hadn't stood up.

"You gonna keep sulking or are you gonna move it?" He unlocked the door, grabbed one of the bars, and pulled. "I don't care either way." Maddock turned and ran up the steps.

"This is a trick, right?"

Maddock opened the wallet and found himself staring at the guard's ID card. According to the card, the man on the deck was called Thomas Thorn, aged thirty-eight, and lived in Germany. He closed the wallet and left the hold, aware that his untrustworthy cellmate wasn't far behind him.

"Found something that belongs to you, Thomas," he said once he'd caught up with the guard. "If you've finished staring, I think we'd better find somewhere marginally safer."

The other man silently took the wallet from Maddock without taking his eyes off the advancing horde of octopuses. "I'm not sure such a thing exists here. This place looks abandoned."

"Yeah, I got that nobody home vibe as well; still, it's better than staying here."

"What about the bad smell?"

Maddock looked over his shoulder. "You're free to go, Blakey. I don't want to see you again, is that clear?"

The little man glared at the pair of them before spinning around and running in the opposite direction.

"Now what, Maddock?"

"Now we go give the people in there the bad news."

The guard nodded. "Something tells me that they already know."

CHAPTER TEN

The Prowler did not snore. He had cured himself of this affliction many years ago back when he went by the name of Fletcher Davis; back when his mum still ruled their massive three bedroomed house in the middle of an isolated woodland on the outskirts of the state of Maine.

That wasn't completely true. It's just that over the years, he'd tried his hardest to flush every hurtful thing she'd inflicted upon his body out of his mind. She'd been the one to stop him from snoring by filling his mouth with toothpaste whenever she caught him doing it. Thinking back, it didn't sound all that cruel but back when he was eight years old. She also held his nose and yelled into his face while he tried not to swallow down all that minty glutinous stuff.

He opened his eyes, grateful that the pitch-black interior of his box wiped away the remaining smoke-like ghosts lingering over from his dream. It had been a long time since she had returned to try and upset him. If The Prowler was in any way superstitious, he would have interpreted what he remembered of his dream as a portent.

The Prowler did not need his over-active mind to lift the rug, exposing a pile of golden coins. No matter what challenges his immediate future would be throwing at him, for the first time since that judge sent him down, The Prowler felt good about himself, even if his body argued otherwise.

He stretched what muscles the confined space allowed then caressed the rough wood on the inside of the box while listening to the sounds coming from the room. He was no longer alone. It was the weird noises coming from beyond the box that had woken him up. The Prowler frowned. What could it be? His imagination showed him hundreds of slugs, each one the size of his arm, crawling up the walls, and over his lid. The Prowler absolutely detested slugs. They were not exactly his favourite creature. He counted to three, swallowed his creeping fear, and pushed open the lid a crack. The picture which assaulted his eyes made him want to slam the lid shut and stay in the darkness for the next week!

Two octopuses, each one the same size as him, were out there. The nearest one was just inches from his box, while the other had taken up position two feet up the wall opposite. Malevolence oozed from every pore of their slimy skins. He wanted to move, but The Prowler dare not even breathe, let alone move; he couldn't stay in here, not with the knowledge of what lay out there. His impetus went into overdrive when a line of muted daylight stung his eyes. The light continued to increase. He slammed a hand over his mouth to stop himself from shrieking when that monster's tentacles pushed the lid up even further.

He threw his body out of the box and scurried on his hands and knees over to the open door, while expecting those thick tentacles to curl around his ankle and drag him back. His terror filled mind screamed out in triumph when he rolled through that opening and to safety. The Prowler rolled onto his back. His last image before he used both feet to kick the door shut was of that octopus sliding out of his box and racing towards him. God almighty, it could move!

He sat up and swapped his feet for his hands. That, without any doubt, had to be the scariest thing that had ever happened to him!

As soon as he opened his lid, that bloody octopus knew that food was just inches from its tentacles. It must have thought the box was his shell. "Oh, Christ," he whispered. "That thing was about to prise me out of that box and dine on my soft bits like I was just another crab!"

The Prowler slowly got to his feet. He knew he wasn't totally safe; how could he be? Those huge octopuses hadn't magically appeared out of thin air; they must have come from somewhere. He turned around.

Both his hands grabbed a support pole when his eyes took in the nightmarish sight beyond the boat. Both the beach and the sea surrounding the island was now black with octopus. There was no way off this vessel without those Lovecraftian monstrosities grabbing him. "I woke too late."

What was he going to do now? They were even in the water around the boat! The Prowler stepped back and saw another one on the deck close to the control room, and two more were on top of the crane, feasting on what was left of the man he'd chained there.

One thing was certain, he couldn't stay where is was. The two in the cabin couldn't get him, but that wouldn't stop their friends. Give it another half hour or so, and this boat would be as black as that beach. The Prowler hurried up the stairs and ran over to the control room, only slowing down when the slimy thing close to him suddenly lifted up three of its tentacles and waved them at him. He wished he had something to use to protect himself. He'd already seen how fast they moved. The knife he had left next to Maddock would come in useful about now.

It was going to charge at him! The Prowler took one step back and got ready to run; he didn't have to go far, just enough for that thing there to lose interest in him.

It lifted one more tentacle into the air. He glanced over his shoulder to ensure that no more were sneaking up on him. When he turned back, every limb was now lying on the deck. The thing looked dead. "What the hell?" He took one careful step forward. "I don't believe this" The very knife which he'd left for Maddock was now sticking out of the creature's body.

"One down, a million more to go!" said a familiar voice.

The Prowler looked up and saw Blakey sitting on the flat roof of the control room.

"Oh, yeah, I plugged it real good there, Fletcher. So," the little man grinned, "looks like you owe me your life." He reached down beside him and lifted up a pistol. "In case you haven't been paying attention, what with you hiding like a big smelly mouse, we're in a bit a situation here. Luckily, at least for me, I have figured a way to get out of here."

"Don't called me by that name ever again, you little toad." Of all the people to meet, why did if have to be him? The Prowler looked back at the crane, noticing that the two octopuses were no longer on there, and neither was the remains of that body.

"I'll call you whatever I want!"

The Prowler shrugged. He refused to let Blakey get under his skin; the man wasn't worth the emotion. All that concerned him right now was if he had rounds for that gun he gripped. "Thinking back, I should have chained you up last night. I almost cringed when that magnificent creature dived out of the water with those huge jaws wide open. Your mate never stood a chance, Blakey. It bit him in half like he was nothing more than a little carrot."

"Shut up."

The Prowler walked forward until he reached the dead octopus. He kinda felt sorry for it now. Nothing deserved to die at the hands of Blakey. "Why don't you come down here and face me like a man?" He grinned up at him. "Or are you too chicken?"

"One more step, and I swear to God I'll put a bullet in your face!" he screamed.

The little man's panicked noise certainly attracted the attention of the few Octopuses still on the boat. "Then you'll be all alone, Blakey. Well, not totally alone, obviously." He nodded at the wet corpse beside his feet. "Have you noticed how they react to noise by any chance?" The Prowler cupped his hands around his mouth. "Dinnertime!" he screamed.

Blakey held the gun in both shaking hands. "Go on, shithead. Do that again. I dare you."

"Will you save the last bullet for yourself, I wonder?" He then rushed forward, grabbed Blakey's foot and pulled. The man screamed again. His trigger finger jerked once, and The Prowler's left ear burned as the bullet passed within millimetres.

"You little shit!" The Prowler savagely twisted the man's foot around, grunting in satisfaction when Blakey screamed out in shock. He dropped the gun on the roof and kicked out with his remaining leg, missing the man's face by inches. Blakey kicked again, and this time, he hit home. The Prowler staggered back and fell over the dead octopus. By the time he managed to regain his balance, Blakey had retrieved his gun and climbed off the roof.

"Move it," he snarled, pressing the muzzle into the back of his neck. Blakey reached down and pulled the knife out of the octopus. "Don't make me tell you twice."

The Prowler sighed heavily before he moved away from the control room. "Do you have a destination in mind, Blakey, or is this going to be a magical mystery tour?" From the painful prod he'd just received, The Prowler guessed that their little chitchat had just come to an end. What a shame the opportunity to wind up Blakey didn't often arise.

Blakey tapped him on the shoulder and pointed over to the jetty where three smaller octopuses had just slipped back into the water. So, the little grease ball wanted him to go that way. Fair enough. He moved his feet in the direction indicated. "Look at them now, Blakey. The gunshot has got them all excited. I'm pretty sure I know what you're planning. I just hope you realise that it isn't going to work."

"Bet your life?" he whispered into his ear. "You see, I've watched them back at the prison. They only go for one person at a time."

He felt the muzzle move down his back, and The Prowler figured he was about to carry out his threat. Three octopuses were already running towards the pair of them. The Prowler knew it was now or never! He spun around, brought his arm up, and swung it out in an arc. His wrist slammed into Blakey's hand. The shock made him drop the gun. The little man snarled in fury and thrust his knife arm forward.

The Prowler had to jump back to avoid Blakey plunging that blade into his guts. The knife missed him, but he was too late to stop the other man jumping forward and slamming his palm into The Prowler's shoulder.

He cartwheeled backwards and fell straight into the moving octopus mass. Two of them slivered up his legs, and each one wrapped their limbs around his arms. Despite the predicament, The Prowler felt no fear. In fact, a great sense of calm settled over him. He watched in amazement as the octopus on his right arm just dropped off and vanished under his companion's slithering legs.

The Prowler found he could now see the sand. They had all moved a few centimetres away from his body. He slowly got to his feet, nodding as the creatures spilled into the space he'd vacated. The remaining octopus on his left arm had yet to leave him. He gently stroked the creature, marvelling at how it felt beneath his fingers. There was so much hidden strength in those muscles, yet it retained a soft texture which reminded him of a woman's inner thigh; it was a surprisingly pleasant experience.

"What the hell is going on?"

The Prowler reluctantly stopped caressing the creature and lifted his arm up above his head. The octopus did not slide down.

He laughed out loud then threw his arm forward. The animal leaped into the air, landed straight in the middle of Blakey's face then wrapped it eight limbs tight around the back of his legs. The sudden movement acted as a catalyst as every nearby animal raced over to the struggling man and attacked him. He fell backwards and vanished under dozens of writhing bodies.

The Prowler leaned down, scooped up the gun, and walked towards the entrance, smiling as all the animals moved out of his way, creating a path for him.

CHAPTER ELEVEN

Her footsteps echoed throughout this level. The metal gantry beneath her feet carried the noise so well. She stopped walking, placed her hands on the railing, and listened. As before, when she'd stopped a few minutes ago, that persistent sound of those slippery things crawling and climbing up the walls below this level reached her ears. She so wanted to start running; to find somewhere in this damn place where she actually felt safe.

Georgia leaned over and looked down into the depths of the blue Atlantic. Somewhere down there had been the resort's control centre where her cache of weapons would be. Oh, Jesus, like she dare swim down there now, not after what had happened to Liam. They were there alright - only it wasn't just one now. She saw three of those things. The mother's calves swam in a tight circle directly below her as if they could sense she was here. She had to keep going; there was no going back now. Georgia was going to seek revenge for the loss of Liam no matter what.

This knife wasn't exactly going to help her, that's for sure! There will be something else in here somewhere. Hell, one of the guests must have had a gun of some kind; of course, they had. Not all of them were genuine businessmen. They all knew that their resort attracted some of the more unsavoury specimens. Crime bosses and their sycophants came here all the time; at least that's the rumour. Not that she had seen any of them but then again, considering she didn't exactly mix with the staff population, this wasn't much of a surprise.

That noise was getting louder. Why couldn't she see any of them? Oh God, their presence was driving her mental! Georgia looked to her left towards her destination. Two hundred yards further down this gantry was a door that would take her straight into the back of a seafood restaurant. From there, she intended to find a route which wasn't flooded that would lead up to the observation gallery. She knew that was always popular with the tourists, which meant a fair amount of them should have been in there when this disaster hit the resort. She hoped to find other survivors.

Where were those bloody animals? It sounded like they were right next to her now. Georgia then just happened to lift her gaze to the ceiling. Her scream bubbled up her throat and erupted out of her mouth at the sight of the largest octopus she had ever clapped eyes on directly above her. She fell back and hit the deck just as it dropped down. Two of its tentacles wrapped around her left ankle, while another three took her other leg. One more reached out and curled around her left wrist.

It wrenched her forward. And Georgia finally saw its mouth and a pale yellow beak-like appendage which opened and closed. She had one chance while it dragged her closer and closer to her demise. Georgia struggled to pull her knife from her pocket with the one remaining limb while desperately avoiding the monsters remaining tentacles. Just as it lifted her off the floor and positioned Georgia above its beak, she managed to pull out the knife, and thrust it down straight into what she hoped would be its brain.

She felt its limbs lose their grip on her legs just before Georgia fell on top of it. She moaned in disgust before rolling off the dead octopus. "You dirty, horrible, bastard thing!" she yelled. Georgia jumped up and tugged the remaining tentacle off her arm before launching her foot into its body.

It took her another moment to realise that it wasn't alone. There were another six crawling up the walls under the canopy; two of them were close to her only way out. "No, you don't," she snarled. Georgia wasn't going to let them cut her off. Not without a fight anyway.

"You had all better stay away from me!" The woman dropped to her knees and slid the soft corpse across the floor towards the railing. It took a single hard push for it to drop through the gap. Georgia stood up and watched it plummet into the water with a mighty splash.

The two Liopleurodon calves immediately fell upon it. Their razor teeth shredded the corpse, turning the water a deep crimson. The two babies took less than a minute to consume their surprise meal, leaving only a few pieces of flesh bobbing up and down in the water.

Georgia saw something down there too. "Oh, you have got to be kidding me."

She had forgotten to pull the knife out of the dead octopus before tipping it over the edge. Those two fiends were now over the railing and were sliding across the gantry and closing in on her position. What was she going to do now?

She hurriedly took off her top. They were still damp from her time in the water. Georgia twirled it around to make a thick rope. She then brought both ends together before running towards that door. They weren't as large as the one she killed, but it wouldn't make all that much difference if their tentacles got a good hold on her legs and arms.

The closest octopus scuttled at her. She screamed abuse at it while slapping it away with her top. She was almost at the door. The other one had climbed the wall until it was about a foot above her head. It ran parallel as she raced for that door. It felt like it knew exactly what she intended to do. How could that be? It was only an animal!

She skidded to a halt, spun around, and ran over to the railing before turning back around. The octopus on the wall had now fallen to the floor. "Ha! You ain't that brainy." She ran straight at it, and at the last second, Georgia dropped her top straight onto it body before jumping over its two uncovered limbs. Georgia got to the door, desperately pulled down the handle, and cried with relief as it opened inwards.

It took her exactly two seconds to slam that door shut. She took a deep breath before turning around. A wall of stainless steel appliances surrounded Georgia. She got her breathing under control, leaned against the door, and listened for anything that might give away the presence of any other living creature. There wouldn't be any Liopleurodons in here, obviously, but there were way too many hiding places in here for her liking. Too many nooks and crannies that could comfortably hide any one of those slimy terrors.

All she heard was the ticking of a clock.

At least she was safe. As far as Georgia was concerned, that accounted for everything right about now. Looking beyond the appliances, metal surfaces, and the storage compartments, Georgia saw her way out of here - an open doorway which, she assumed, would lead into the main restaurant area. There were no other exits.

Georgia wrapped her arms around her waist. Now that the adrenaline had seeped away, she felt really cold. She stopped beside one of the surfaces. Maybe it was the shock of what she'd just lived through buggering up her internal temperature? There was nothing in here which she could use to cover herself, although Georgia did find something that might come in useful.

She walked between the surfaces and stopped to scoop up a large cleaver. She smiled to herself. Yeah, this would do the job just fine. If any more of those octopuses tried to tangle with her, she'd chop them all up, all ready to be made into calamari. Georgia reached the exit and peered around the corner.

For the first time since losing Liam, she didn't want to meet up with anybody; at least not until she'd made herself decent again. The very image of her bumping into some other survivor with her bits almost on display made her want to laugh at the absurdity of it. Not that it would happen as there was a rather fetching green blouse lying on a table close to the door. Georgia ran in and grabbed it, then poured herself into it, while trying not to think of the fate of the poor woman who had this before her.

There were clothes everywhere. But no sign of anybody living. Judging by the amount of clothing, watches, phones, wallets, and purses strewn around the restaurant, this place must have been packed. She wandered between the tables, kicking away socks and panties, while her mind bombarded her with images of what these poor people must have gone through when the octopuses attacked them. It didn't make any sense; why didn't they just leave?

The question stayed a mystery until she walked past an upturned table and reached the door. She turned the handle and found it locked. What was this, a restaurant lock in? She peered through the window and saw something else which didn't make sense. Not only was the door locked, somebody had bolted the door from the outside. Somebody had made sure that these people wouldn't be able to leave here in a hurry. So where were their attackers? Surely, they couldn't all be still in here.

"In here with me?"

Georgia slowly turned around and scanned the room, looking out for movement. There wasn't anything in here; this place was dead. She walked over to a loose pile of grey clothing and pushed her foot through the material. Some silver coins fell out of one of the pockets, as well as something which could prove useful if she could find the rest of it. Georgia leaned down, pushed the coins aside, and picked up the gun clip. "I knew it!" she muttered triumphantly.

It took Georgia another few moments of searching through the rest of the nearby clothes to find the gun which belonged to the clip. She pushed the magazine into the bottom of the handle and smiled to herself. Now she was ready for that monster.

As she moved away from the table, Georgia's foot caught the edge of a pair of trousers. There was something else down there. She leaned down, hoping to find another magazine; instead, Georgia uncovered a shotgun.

"You are kidding me!" she uttered, lifting the weapon off the floor. She carefully placed it on the table. Although this had to be the best thing she'd found so far, Georgia couldn't help but wonder why the original owner hadn't used them on their attackers. There was no shell damage or blood anywhere in here. It made her wonder if they even worked.

Georgia then remembered her earlier encounter on that gantry and shuddered at the thought of what would have happened if she hadn't looked up. She gazed towards the restaurant ceiling and saw thin green metal pipes running the length of the area. It didn't take her long to realise that those monsters would have dropped en masse onto the faces of the people sat at these tables. None of them would have stood a chance. Even if a couple of them had managed to steer clear of the octopuses, they wouldn't have been able to get very far, not with that door locked and bolted.

She tucked the pistol next to the cleaver, picked up the shotgun, and returned to the restaurant door, wondering how to get through without resorting to blasting her way out. Georgia picked up a chair, lifted it over her head, and flung it straight art the window, shouting in victory when the glass shattered.

"There we go," she said. "That's how you do it!" Georgia walked through the broken glass and hurried over to the shop on the opposite side. This, too, was a restaurant, and just like the one she'd left, this door had been bolted. She peered through the window, sighing in sadness at all the discarded items which lay across the tables and the floor. It would have been so nice to find just one person in there sitting at a table. It would have given her a reason to enter the restaurant. She turned away. Apart from company, everything she needed was either in her hands or tucked into her belt.

The observation lounge wasn't far from here. In fact, the designers had made it a doddle to travel from this eating hub all the way up to the lounge. Obviously, they would pass a number of exclusive clubs before getting there. She walked past the restaurant while listening for any sound that might give away the location of anybody else. Georgia decided not to go into any of the clubs she was approaching. Even though she'd tooled herself up, the prospect of running into anymore of those slimy monsters still filled her with dread. At least out here, she had a clear view. None of them would be able to sneak up on her ever again. Even the ceiling was nice and smooth.

She reached the door of the first club. Just like the restaurants, somebody had bolted the door shut. Georgia stopped walking. The fact that someone had done this was disturbing enough, but what made her question her memory was that she'd walked along this route loads of time and never once noticed any bolts on the doors before. For one thing, they were fire-exits, so they shouldn't have had them fixed in the first place.

Georgia really should unbolt that door and open it just in case anybody was still trapped in there, but no matter how hard she tried, the mental image of her pulling open that door and finding herself buried under a dozen of those vile animals wouldn't leave her alone. Once again, she cursed her vivid imagination before hurrying to the next club before her cowardice really took hold.

The next club, called The Last Mermaid, wouldn't cause any trouble for her bravery as the door was wide open. She still didn't enter, namely because she had just encountered her first octopus since leaving the gantry. This one was well and truly dead.

Even this made her frown, as it was pinned to the open door. Somebody had shot it with either a bolt gun or crossbow. The thin metal spike pierced its body and the wood. She knew there were no weapons like this on the resort, at least not in the official inventory. There were a few spearguns, but nothing which used bolts.

Not that it meant much. The weapons in her possession weren't exactly official either, but since when did questionable gentlemen with money go around with bolt-guns or crossbows? Georgia closed the door, noticing that the bolt had gone straight through the other side. She also saw that there was no bolt on this door either. "Weirder and weirder," she muttered.

Georgia hurried passed the next three clubs, not daring to stop of even turn to look in case she saw anything else unexplained. All that mattered was to reach that lounge. From there, she'd have the best view in the resort; not only did it show over half the resort's walkways, it also showed her the jetty where the passengers boarded the departing ships. If there were anybody left, that had to be the place where there'd go.

She walked up a flight of ornate marble steps while listening to the gentle trickle of the twin miniature water features at either side of the step. It so helped to calm her frayed nerves. The noise of the water droplets sliding over the spherical, silver statues sounded like most natural thing in here.

The bay window which displayed the outside was on the level above this one. Georgia walked through the display of tropical trees, keeping to the stone path. It made her feel so much better to see no clothing anywhere around here. Apart from a couple of Coke cans and an empty champagne flute stood on a stone plaque in the middle of the display, Georgia saw nothing out of place. She laid the shotgun down on a picnic table and approached the window that showed her the floor below.

Just like the restaurants, she saw items of clothing as well as other pieces of personal possessions, but still no people. It couldn't be possible that only she had survived this catastrophe, and yet it really did begin to look that way.

She made her way up to the next level, praying that the jetty was going to prove her wrong.

"Oh, my God!"

There was a large ship out there! That couldn't be possible. No ship was due to dock at the resort for another day, and that decrepit old wreck out there certainly wasn't it. She noticed movement. Georgia ran to the window, pressed her face against the glass, and watched in utter horror as three women raced along the jetty and onto the ship. As soon as they were aboard, over twenty small octopuses dropped on their heads.

"Oh, God. Please, make this nightmare end!"

That ship was overrun with them. They were everywhere.

She spun around when she heard footsteps. Three men were walking towards her. The middle one held a shotgun. It took her moments to realise that was the one she'd left on that table; it also took her the same amount of time to realise that they weren't guests either. The prison uniforms were a big giveaway.

"Well, ain't you a pretty one," said the large, bald man in the middle. He nodded to the other two who rushed towards her.

They took Georgia's knife and pistol before returning to the man holding her shotgun.

"Now, I wonder what we should do with you?"

Their leering eyes rode up and down her body, making her believe that looking for other people might have been the worst mistake of her life. If they hadn't removed her weapons, Georgia would have considered making a run for it. After all, at least she knew where she stood with an octopus.

CHAPTER TWELVE

Christ, where had that guard gone to?

He spun his head away from the entrance to the kiddie playground when an ominous shadow blocked out most of the daylight. Maddock pulled his arms back through the mangled steel mesh and swallowed down the frantic urge to bellow out when the owner of that shadow swam towards him.

There was no escape, no way out, nothing to stop that monster from turning him into flesh confetti. Maddock kept perfectly still, not even daring to breath while the ancient marine nightmare swam straight past him, its huge oar-shaped rear limb brushing past his chest. How had it not seen him?

The huge animal swam towards where Maddock wanted to go before performing a graceful upward lunge towards the surface. He then noticed movement; there was an octopus on the wall about a foot above the water's surface. It scuttled down the wall and stopped beside what looked like a metal bench.

He knew that staying here would be suicide. That whale-sized monster must hast sensed him even inside this wetsuit. Maddock's muscles refused to move, until he witnessed this. The monster pushed its vast bulk out of the water and snapped the unsuspecting creature straight off the wall before falling back. The octopus never stood a chance.

The monster turned away from Maddock, and he decided that getting the hell out of here would be best decision of his life. He wouldn't be able to go up there, though, that's for sure. Not with that thing hanging around.

Maddock did bellow out when something tapped him on the shoulder. A narrow column of bubbles shot out of Maddock's rebreather and rose until they burst against the bottom of the monster's tail. He moaned in terror as he watched it literally spin on itself and dive back down heading straight for Maddock. Its jaws opened wide, displaying a mouthful of teeth, each one the size of a kitchen knife.

A gloved hand grabbed Maddock's arm and pulled him backwards, away from the approaching monster and into a narrow corridor. The grip around his arm vanished. He turned and discovered the prison guard frantically gesticulating behind his faceplate. He pointed over Maddock's shoulder and then at an open door not far from where they were. He turned around and forced down another scream when he saw that the corridor was narrow, and the monster was still coming after them!

Maddock rolled back around and followed his companion towards that open door, acutely aware of that nightmare desperately trying to force its shoulders past the concrete walls. From the jolting vibrations and the noise, that thing was succeeding as well. He swam as fast as he could, expecting to feel the agonising crunch of that monster's jaw cutting him in two any second. That door was literally seconds away when he dared to look over his shoulder. Those walls stood no chance against that animal's determination to catch its next meal. Its bulk had demolished both sides!

Its jaw was already open wide and ready to bite down on his legs, when a volley of bolts sped through the clear water, and punched into the monster's flesh. The guard pulled Maddock backwards, through the open door, and over towards a flight of steps.

Maddock grabbed the first step and scrambled up and pushed himself out of the water. He rolled onto his back and pulled the mask off his face and took in a huge lungful of air.

"Oh shit, oh shit, oh shit," he panted. "I thought I was a goner just then. Did you see how fast it moved?"

"Shut up, Maddock, and get up!"

He looked back towards the water and groaned at the sight of that dark shadow rushing towards them at high speed. Maddock managed to get to his feet and race towards a set of double doors. He got there just as the animal burst out of the water. It picked up Maddock's faceplate and swallowed it before sliding back under the water.

"Well done, Maddock. If you were a cat, you'd only have eight more lives left."

He sank to the floor and rested his back against the side of the door frame after double checking that the monster really had left them. Christ on a bike, that was a close one. He lifted his hands up in front of his face and wiggled his fingers.

"What are you doing."

"Making sure all my extremities are where they should be." He ran his fingers down his cheeks, feeling the wet stubble under the digits. How long had it been since he'd had a shave? Maddock felt the sudden need to laugh out loud. Of all the random things to think about at a time like this! "Where were you, man?" Maddock took a deep breath. "I thought you were right behind me." His racing heart refused to slow down. That had to rate as the most terrifying experience of his life. The octopuses were bad enough that that thing truly had emerged from some psycho's insane nightmare.

"That's the weird thing, Maddock. You see, I thought I was behind you." Thomas patted the top of the black weapon he held. "It's only when the figure I was following turned and fired a bolt at me with this that I figured not everything was right with this picture."

The prison guard offered Maddock the weapon.

"Wait, so you ended up following some other guy?"

"Same body mass, wearing the same colour wetsuit and rebreather." Thomas shrugged. "I guess stuff like this happens all the time. So, it turns out that we weren't all alone down here after all, and he isn't all too friendly."

"Yeah. This is getting weirder by the minute. Do you think he could be one of The Beast's guys?"

Thomas shook his head. "Not a chance. I know the lunks who grease around him. They're all violent idiots. The guy in the wetsuit knew what he was doing.

Maddock turned the weapon around, looking for any distinguishing marks like a maker's stamp. He found nothing at all. It must be something made for the resort; something the staff used to protect themselves when venturing outside. "Where did the other guy go?"

Thomas shook his head. "I thought he went this way. It's difficult to make out. He took off after he dropped the gun in the water, and I realised that you were in trouble. Makes sense that he came this way. I mean, I didn't see any other exits, did you?"

"Sorry, mate. I was too busy crapping myself to notice." He forced his attention back to the weapon. The magazine held about thirty steel bolts. Maddock guessed that ten was missing. He frowned. Where did the cylinder go? It had to be gas powered. Either that or there was a thick elastic band somewhere inside it.

He looked up and nodded at Thomas. "For the life in me, I can't figure out why he fired at you. Also, what was he doing in the water in the first place. It wouldn't take any survivor that long to realise that the water was the last place to enter."

"It's pretty hard to mistake me for an octopus."

"Not enough limbs for a start."

Even with the gun's reassuring weight, there wasn't a chance in hell that he was going anywhere near that water again - meaning they'd need to find another way through the resort. This could be problematic. As far as they could work out, swimming through the flooded school and up into a gymnasium was their only way out of here. Maddock followed his colleague's gaze down the dark corridor. From here, he saw a number of octopuses silvering up and down the walls.

"Considering how close we came to getting eaten, I don't think we should follow our planned route."

"Oh, you think?"

"This place is a bloody maze. Didn't the guys who designed this place ever think of putting up a few signs? Still, it's not like we're totally out of options." He zipped down the inside of his wetsuit and pulled out a couple of cell phones that he'd picked up close to the entrance. "Great. Still no signal. You know, the longer I'm here the more I wish I'd found somewhere at the prison to hide. I'd be safely in a helicopter on my way to a hot shower, decent food, and a clean bed by now."

"Yeah, and if I'd done that, I'll either be back in a cell, or your pals would have shot me just on general principle." He laughed. "Ain't weird how things turn out? I mean, I intended to try to help out my fellow cell-mates, and look how well that went."

Maddock brushed past the guard and waited for one of those animals at the back of the corridor to notice him. It didn't take long. One of them leapt off the floor and raced along the wall, heading towards him at high speed. Maddock waited for a few more seconds before lifting the gun, taking aim, and squeezing the trigger. One bolt left the barrel at high speed and almost split the animal's body in half when it sliced through its flesh.

"It's almost as if this weapon was designed solely for killing these nightmares." He gazed steadily at Thomas. "We do make a good team."

"That we do, Maddock. The prison guard and the prisoner working together to defeat killer octopuses." He grinned. "Sounds like the description of a really bad movie."

"Hell, I'd watch it. I used to love stuff like that." Maddock looked down at the thing he'd just killed. "I guess you still intend to find the other prisoners and stop them? Although I'm not too sure how we're going to accomplish that one short of killing them."

"I have no other choice, Maddock. It's my duty. I know most of the other guards didn't really believe in their work, but I do."

"Hey, don't sweat it. I don't want those goons walking about either. Hell, they give our species a bad name."

Thomas took a couple of tentative steps towards the water, lapping over the top step. "I can't see your friend, Maddock."

"No, and I can't see your friend either. Makes you wonder how the man was able to get past all those things in front of us."

Thomas shrugged. "We can ask him that when we catch up to him. Now, either kill those bloody things, or give me the gun back so I can kill the bastards.

"I got this, Thomas." He walked over to the wall and slapped his hand against it. "Hello there, slimeballs! Come on over here. The winner gets a nice big chocolate cake." The four remaining octopuses raced along the wall. It took him just moments to wipe them out. "No chocolate for any of you lot," he said, walking over the first one he'd killed. "Do you see what I mean now? This device was made to kill these horrible things. They go together like strawberries and cream."

Thomas pushed past him and covered the distance between Maddock and the end of the corridor in seconds. He stepped over the octopuses corpses and reached for the handle. "What is it with you and food, man?"

Maddock's smart reply lodged in his throat when the man pulled open the door and several more of the slimy nightmares fell on Thomas. Their tentacles wrapped around every part of his body. He dare not shoot for fear of hitting him! He dropped the gun and dug his fingers into the body of the closest animal. Cringing as its sloppy inside shot up his arm. It felt like he'd just plunged his hand into a bucket of warm raw liver.

Thomas writhed and bucked while trying desperately to pull the things off him, but the man was obviously fighting a losing battle. As soon as he pulled off one tentacle, another three took its place. "Use your knife!" shouted Maddock. He reached out and grabbed one which had slivered up Thomas's shoulder. It was trying to reach the man's face. Maddock clenched his fingers, grinning in satisfaction at the sound of its slimy flesh ripping. "Yeah, you like that don't you!"

His colleague had managed to pull the knife out of his belt and had already shredded two more of them. He scurried backwards and got to his feet with the remaining animal still clinging onto his left arm. The man growled then slammed it into the wall.

Maddock scooped up the gun when he saw another three of them scurrying towards them. He took them out before any of the things got close. "You okay?"

Thomas stood just behind him, panting heavily. He nodded before slumping against the wall. "I think we're gonna need another one of those," he said, pointing at the bolt-gun. "More ammo, too, I reckon." He savagely kicked the closest corpse before striding purposefully down the dark corridor. "Are you coming then or what?"

"Are you sure you're going to be okay? At least let me have a look at your arm."

Thomas obviously had no intention of listening to him. Maddock inwardly sighed while he removed the magazine and tried to work out how many bolts he had let. Thomas was right about the ammo thing, there wasn't that many left.

"Do you want me to stay here while you open that door again, man?" He waited for him to slow down and stop. "Your friend is either immune to these things, or he's gone another route because he couldn't have come this way."

"You think there's a hidden door somewhere?"

Maddock laughed. "Now you're thinking like me!" He walked over to him and gently wrapped his fingers around the man's wrists then rolled the suit fabric up his arm. "Shit." Ugly red circular welts covered skin all the way up to Thomas's shoulder.

"I think my legs are the same, too. They itch like a bastard, but they don't hurt. I think the wetsuit protected me from the worst of it, Maddock." He rolled the sleeve down. "That's twice you've saved my life."

"Yeah, it's becoming a bit of a habit, man."

Maddock looked back at the trail of corpses they left and felt himself go cold at just how different the last few minutes could have been if either of them had agreed to split up earlier. It also made him think hard about what else could be waiting for them down here. He knew for a fact that they hadn't seen the last of these nightmares.

Was there really a hidden door back there? If there was, the implications were utterly terrifying. He forced that from his mind, deciding not to think about it. Right now, the pair of them needed to get out of here; to find some kind of safety, if such a thing existed. Maddock didn't think his colleague was as okay as he pretended to be. He'd seen the similar kind of symptoms back when he served. The terror and stress had seeped into the man's bones.

"Are you ready to go on, Maddock?"

He nodded and gently patted Thomas on the shoulder. "Yeah, let's do this. This time, I'll go first okay?"

"I ain't going to complain at that."

"No, I didn't think you would." Maddock ran over to the next door and pressed his ear against the surface. He couldn't hear anything on the other side. Perhaps lady luck had decided to stop being a bitch to them for a few minutes?" He looked back, and Thomas and winked. "I think we're going to be okay."

Watching the guard take a couple of steps back didn't exactly fill Maddock with confidence. Before his nerve broke, Maddock wrenched the door open then jumped back, fully expecting an onslaught of a dozen waving tentacles ready to wrap around his face. All he received as the door bounced off the wall was a faint odour of rotting seaweed. The light wasn't great, but he could see that nothing ahead moved.

"Are we safe?"

"Looks like it." Maddock leaned forward, trying to make out if there was another door at the end of the next corridor. "This is ridiculous," he muttered. Maddock ran forward a couple of metres, passing by a complicated network of thin metal pipes bolted to both walls. There were two ladders, one on each side; the left one dropped down to the level below. Thanks to that monster eating his rebreather, Maddock wouldn't be able to follow that route. The ladder on the other side looked more promising as that one led to the floor above.

He waited for Thomas to catch up before tapping the ladder on the right. "There's one route out. Fancy taking it?" he suggested.

Thomas pointed forward. "Let's see where this leads first."

"Any particular reason?"

He pointed at the floor. "Yeah, there's footsteps leading that way." Thomas grinned. "I reckon the bastard who took a pot shot at me went this way."

"Fair enough." Maddock took a couple of steps forward. He now saw the wet prints on the floor and wondered why the hell he hadn't noticed them first. He must be getting slow in his old age. His eyesight might not be as keen as it once was, but Maddock's hearing certainly hadn't diminished. He skidded to an abrupt stop. "What was that?"

"What? All I can hear is you." replied Thomas. "Oh, wait." He urgently tapped Maddock's left shoulder. "Fuck, over there! Oh Hell!"

Maddock took his eyes off the floor, looked at the walls, and immediately wished he hadn't! Dozens of octopuses covered both walls and the ceiling, and all of them were scuttling towards them. Their shining, writhing forms completely covered the surfaces, making it look as though a single organism of pulsating, black jelly was rushing forward.

He spun around and raced back, trying to keep hold of the gun as he stumbled and tripped on the trail of wet corpses he'd already left. Maddock only realised after they ran past the ladder that the pair of them were running into a dead end! He risked a look behind his shoulder and moaned in horror at that bubbling mass of limbs and suckers. The vile nightmares were gaining on them!

They both burst into the last room. "Thomas, you can save yourself! Go on, get the hell out of here."

He shook his head. "No, I'm not leaving you here." Come on Maddock, we'll just have to share the mask." Thomas ran over to the steps. He looked over his shoulder. "Hurry up. They're almost on us."

Maddock yelped out in terror at the sight of that huge familiar shadow behind the guard. He ran over to him and pulled him away just in time as the monster had reappeared. Only, it didn't seem to care about the two humans. The beast pulled its huge bulk up the stairs until its front limbs rested on the top step. Maddock pushed himself into the corner of the room and slammed a hand over his mouth to stop himself from screaming when its massive jaws opened. They were both within easy reach of the monster.

The foul stench of rotting meat filled the room as it swung that head from side to side. Thomas did release a muffled moan when the octopuses scuttled out of the corridor and spread out along the walls. The monster wasted no time in lunging forward and picking them off the surfaces one by one. Its front teeth easily pulled them away before it opened its jaws and swallowed them whole.

Its ravenous appetite seemed impossible to quench. Dozens of them succumbed to those jaws, but a few octopuses were now managing to get past the animal and escape into the water behind the wall. The flow now began to ebb until only a couple of strays were left. By this time, the huge marine predator was slowing down. Of the three which entered the room, it only managed to catch one octopus.

Maddock watched it slowly push it bulk back into the water. He waited until it was out of sight before remembering to breathe. He peeled his back off the wall and got to his feet while keeping his eyes fixed on those steps. Maddock pressed a finger to his lips before slowly edging along the wall, heading towards the corridor.

Once the pair of them had passed through the double doors, Maddock finally took his gaze away from the water and looked forward. Apart from numerous puddles of water left by the octopuses, he saw no movement. "I really do think we've overstayed our welcome, Thomas."

His colleague managed a single shaky nod. He looked as white as a sheet. Maddock guessed that he probably looked the same.

"What did we just witness?"

"Who the hell cares?" he snapped. "Come on, let's get a move on.!" He raced down the corridors and headed for that ladder on the right. The quicker he got out of here, the better he'd feel. It wasn't until his fingers wrapped around the cold metal when it clicked that the corpses had vanished. "Shut up, Maddock," he whispered. "Focus on the now."

He moved to the side. "You know what? Screw this. You can go first this time, Thomas." He passed him the gun."

"I still think we should keep going forward. There can't be any of those things left now."

Maddock shook his head. "I'm not betting our lives on it, mate." He suddenly held up his hand, spotting Thomas's protest before it began. He could hear a noise. It sounded like an octopus but... He shook his head in confusion. No, the noise wasn't right.

"What the hell is that noise?" hissed Thomas.

"Climb, man. Climb!" He'd figured it out. Maddock had also worked out why the octopuses charged down here. They weren't after them, they were running away from something! They jumped onto the ladders just as a tentacle as thick as his thigh snaked across the floor. Maddock reached the top, barely noticing their new surroundings. He grabbed Thomas's arm and pulled him as far away from the hatch as he could.

"What? What was it?"

Maddock, shook his head. "You really don't want to know."

Thomas tapped him on the shoulder. "Oh, well, there's a piece of good news. Look who I spot!"

He followed the guard's gaze and saw their quarry. Three prisoners as well as somebody else. It looked like a blonde woman, and from where they stood, it was obvious that she was in distress!

CHAPTER THIRTEEN

She had never seriously believed in fate. What little faith she had in the concept of destiny went out of the window back in her teenage years when her parents died in a car accident. Her notion of luck died back then, too.

Until a moment ago, her belief remained dead. The three men had finished playing. The thin veneer of mock civility faded to nothing with naked lust now taking its place. What stopped them in their tracks as well as reigniting her faith was the sudden presence of another two men running towards them.

It took her seconds to register that the new arrivals were a threat to the three men. She acted in instinct alone and snatched her pistol from out of the prisoner's belt. Her motion did not go unnoticed, only she was ready this time. As soon as the man spun around, Georgia launched her left foot up between his legs. He collapsed like a wet paper bag. Her gun was already aimed at the fat man's face before his undamaged spare goon could bring up her stolen shotgun.

Georgia didn't need to utter a word of warning. The first stranger to reach them wrenched the shotgun out of the astonished man's grip and pointed the business straight at his face.

The groaning man in front of her still hadn't taken the hint. He swept his arm out, trying to grab her ankle. She neatly sidestepped his attempt then used her foot the push him back onto the floor. He landed on his front. Georgia dropped both knees hard on his spine and pushed the muzzle into the back of his neck. "Go on, move again, give me a reason to blow your head off."

They both looked to be in their early thirties, both over six foot, and both wearing their recent experiences in their facial expressions. The blonde one who'd snatched the shotgun crouched in front of the sprawled man. Georgia started when she noticed the prison collar peeking out from under the wetsuit.

"Oh, don't be too concerned about the threads. Believe me, I've nothing to do with these losers. It's just that some people high up took a dislike to my pretty face and framed me for a crime I didn't do."

"Yeah, you're innocent," sniggered the man under Georgia's knees. "We're all innocent."

The new arrival crouched down. "Shut up, Bates. You were born evil." He pressed the gun against the back of his head. "Only reason why I don't kill you here and now is because I don't want to mess up the pretty woman's clothes." He stood up and took his hand from the underside of the gun. The new arrival held out his hand. "My name is Maddock." he gently grasped her hand, "and it's a genuine pleasure to actually meet up with a friendly face."

"I'm Georgia," she replied.

"The worm who you so expertly put on the floor is called Ryan Bates. He likes to cut things off people. He isn't a nice man." Maddock nodded over to the other man. "He's called Thomas. That guy is going to remove these vile individuals from your resort, miss, and put them back inside a cell."

The fat man laughed out loud.

"He likes the others to called him The Beast, but his real name is Clarence Stuger. The little guy next to him, the one who looks a bit like a beetle, is called Harry Morris." He tipped an imaginary hat over to the other men. "Enjoy your brief stay outside, fellas!"

"That's ain't gonna happen." Ryan lifted his head. "You'll see as soon as your back's turned. Once you think you're safe and cosy, I'm gonna come after you first, lovely Georgia." He licked his lips. "I'm so gonna enjoy cutting bits off your epic body; see if I don't."

Georgia leaned closer to the prisoner. "You talk too much." She slammed her palm into the back of his head. Ryan cried out in pain when his forehead smacked against the floor.

"'I'm going to kill you for that!" he snarled, savagely twisting his body. Ryan bucked and threw the woman off him, but before he could carry out his threat, Maddock cracked the man with the shotgun butt.

"Enough!" growled Maddock.

The other guy, the one in the uniform, ordered the other two prisoners to lie on their fronts. "You okay over there, Maddock?"

"Yeah. It's all peachy," he replied, winking at Georgia.

"Gonna cut you good," murmured Ryan.

"I told you to keep quiet."

Georgia considered kicking the bastard this time. Her decision to hurt him again quickly came to a halt when he gave her a vile grin accompanied by his fat tongue running along his mouth. Yet before she was able to put the boot in, the other man, Clarence, got there first and ordered him to act like a gentleman in front of the lady. She honestly thought he was taking the piss until she looked sharply at the fat man, only to find his gaze fixed upon something else. Georgia followed the direction towards the hole where the two men had emerged. There was something else down there, and it sure as hell wasn't human!

"Fellas. I believe I should apologise for the rather excitable behaviour of my colleagues," said Clarence. "Right now, it might be a wise idea to put aside our acrimonious relationship for the present, work as a team, and help each other find a way out of here."

"You have got to be joking, Clarence! Work as a team?" Maddock laughed. "Not a chance. I wouldn't trust you and your monkeys as far as I could throw a filthy bath slopping over with thick grease."

"You take that that back, Maddock" snarled the little man sitting next to The Beast. "The boss keeps his word, and you know it."

It was another one of those vile animals, but this octopus was no lightweight. Georgia silently moaned as one of its tentacles rose up through the hole, the limb was as thick as her leg. It carried on rising all the way up to the ceiling before the tip flattened out against the surface. The limb slowly rotated until she saw the double row of suction cups running all the way down its limb. Georgia slowly moved back, unable to move her head away from the terrifying sight happening just a few feet away from them.

"I'll let that insult pass, Maddock, for the sake of our future friendship. I promise that neither of my colleagues will misbehave. Of course, you could just stand there and keep shaking your head. That's cool with me as it probably means that that pet you brought with you will eat your worthless bodies first."

The tentacle had located a thick metal pole embedded in the ceiling. It curled the tip around the pole and pulled on it. Georgia tapped Maddock on the shoulder. "I think you should listen to him," she said. Another limb was trying, without much success, to squeeze through the hole. "We need to get out of here!"

Maddock took her hand then slowly pulled Georgia away. "I think we're okay. Looks like it's stuck."

A loud grinding noise made her cry out in surprise, and then the whole floor around the hole bulged up. Fine cracks sped out from the hole, and the surrounding concrete began to crumble and shift as the second limb rose.

"We need to get out of here!" shouted Ryan.

Georgia snatched her hand out of Maddock's grasp and raced over to the nearest door. She pulled it open and pressed her back against the surface. "This way," she shouted.

Maddock pulled Ryan up and pushed the shotgun into the man's back. "You heard the lady. Shift it!"

Three tentacles were now anchored on that pole and were trying to pull the rest of the animal's bulk through the rapidly disintegrating hatchway. Both Ryan, Maddock, and Thomas had already passed her when one of those incredibly long limbs detached from the pole and dropped to the floor, narrowly missing Clarence's other minion by inches.

He shrieked out in shock. Georgia swallowed hard as the tentacle flicked across the floor, heading straight for the door.

"Come on, Chubby!" yelled Maddock. "Get those legs moving."

Once the remaining men were safely through, Georgia slammed the door and rammed home both bolts. She almost bit her tongue in fright when the limb bashed against the door.

"Jesus," she murmured. "Just how big are they going to get?"

"Madam. My gratitude for your quick thinking. You saved our lives." Clarence performed a mock bow.

"Give it up, Clarence," snapped Thomas. "Your theatrics aren't fooling anybody. We all know that if we hadn't taken the guns, you'd have left us two and the girl back there as bait for that thing."

Clarence smiled. "Thomas, you have hurt my feelings. I certainly wouldn't have abandoned the pretty lady."

"Whatever." The prison guard walked up to Georgia. "Thanks." He then lifted up the gun he'd brought with him. "Do you recognise this by any chance?"

She took the weapon from his hands. "What does it fire?"

"Solid metal bolts."

Georgia remembered the octopus she passed skewered to the wall. "No. They're not part of the resort's inventory."

"Okay, not to worry." Thomas glanced across at Maddock. "This is your territory, so do you know if there's a transmitter anywhere?"

"There's probably one in the control , but that area is flooded. There's no way to reach it."

"Oh, come on, don't give me that," snapped Clarence. "It isn't the 20th century anymore. All we have to do is look for a cell phone. There's bound to be a few scattered around here somewhere."

Thomas reached inside his pocket, brought out a phone and threw it at the fat man. "There you go, chunky. You try and get an outside signal, and before you ask, yes I have found others and they're all the bloody same."

That last statement effectively knocked off the fat man's permanent sneer. He didn't even examine the cell phone. Clarence now looked truly terrified. It didn't last, though; his fear quickly vanished under that returning look of smugness.

"Fine, so we can't radio for help," continued Thomas. "Okay then, miss, is there another way off this island? An alternative port perhaps?"

Georgia nodded. "Yeah, there's another freight route at the far end of the island, Thomas. I'm not sure if a boat is berthed, though, and even if it is, there's nowhere to go once we leave."

"It's the best we have," said Maddock. "Let's be honest here. It can't be any worse that staying here."

Georgia opened her mouth to argue the point then abruptly shut it after Maddock gave her such a weird look. "Can you lead the way, Georgia?"

"I guess so." She shuffled them all along and hurried towards the observation deck, but before she reached it, Georgia took an abrupt left turn, and lead them through a fire exit and down a flight of metal step. She stopped a couple of steps from the bottom when she noticed the water. "Damn it." She moved to the side. "Looks like we're going to get our feet wet."

"Where does this lead?" asked Maddock.

"There's a casino beyond that door. This is the quickest way to the port on the other side. At least, it's the only way I know that won't involve swimming." Georgia splashed down the last two steps and grabbed hold of the door handle.

"Wait!" cried Thomas. He pushed passed the others and levelled his gun at the door. He looked at Georgia and gave her a single nod.

What had these two gone through to take such extreme precautions against a closed door? She then remembered the situation that Thomas and Maddock found herself in and wondered whether, if she'd taken a few more precautions, then those prisoners wouldn't have gotten the upper hand. Georgia slowly pulled the door open. Apart from a plastic casino chip floating through the gap, nothing jumped out at them.

"Follow me," she said, wading through the open door. It didn't surprise her to find the casino devoid of people. Thankfully, the same applied to the octopus invasion as well. Georgia stopped beside a roulette wheel and looked around the ornate room. The designers had attempted to recreate this establishment in the style of a casino from the late 19th century complete with framed pictures of American outlaws adorning the walls. The staff here were forced to wear period costumes that itched like hell. At least that's what, Donna, one of her friends complained about.

Georgia looked at the wooden balcony which enclosed the casino. There were several rooms up there; could Donna or anybody else be up there? They sure as hell wouldn't stay down here in this ankle-deep cold water.

"Where now, Georgia?"

She pointed towards the large entrance at the front of the room. "We just go straight through, Thomas. Wait a minute first." Before anyone could respond or try to stop her, Georgia ran over to the staircase, and raced up the steps. She ran over to the first room and peered inside. Her heart sank at the sight of a casino uniform piled in an untidy heap in the corner of the room. "Oh, shit, not Donna as well." So those vile slimy bastards had been in here after all. Georgia checked all the other rooms and found crumpled clothes in there too.

Georgia left the balcony and returned to the others, feeling like she's just been smacked in the guts. Then again, what else had she expected? She had to face the simple truth: that she was the only survivor.

"I'm sorry, Georgia," said Maddock.

"Look, are we going to stay here all day? I'm kinda eager to find somewhere dry."

She glared at Ryan. "There's plenty of empty rooms up there. Why don't you go take a little nap?"

"Only if you're going to join me, darling," he replied, winking.

"I thought you said your men were going to behave?"

"Cool your jets, Mr Prison Officer. It's only a bit of light-hearted banter." Clarence bowed again. "Miss, if you've quite finished having a bit of a wander, perhaps we can get on? Unless you wanted to give us a guided tour of the restrooms first."

Georgia felt herself colouring up. She waded past the men while silently wishing that either Thomas or Maddock would get so annoyed with the fat man's continuous mock civility that they'd shut him up permanently. Maybe she'd get lucky, and an octopus might drop on his head. She'd quite happily stand back and watch it kill him as well. Oh, Christ, what was with her? Since when did wishing death upon another human being, even one as vile as Clarence, become normal?

She walked up the gentle ramp and through the casino doors, thankful that the water here only reached above her shoes. As she reached the next junction, she became aware of a presence beside her. She saw Maddock's sad smile and just knew that he was about to ask if she was feeling okay. Like she needed that right now.

"What did you find in those rooms, Georgia?"

"What?"

The rooms above the casino. Something startled you, Georgia."

"It's probably nothing."

"Your body language said otherwise. It's okay, you can tell me."

"I have a friend who worked here, and I found her clothing in one of the rooms."

"I don't understand how this could upset you."

"Haven't you seen the clothing piles?"

Maddock shrugged. "Probably, but then again, I've seen a lot of stuff in here, and obviously not all of it has had time to register." He leaned closer. "I take it you know the reason?"

Why was she finding it so difficult to continue? Georgia took a deep breath. "It's those octopuses. It's how they feed. They inject an enzyme into your body which liquidise your interactive organs, and then they suck out the mush."

"That's disgusting," Maddock replied. "It still doesn't fully explain your friend's disappearance. If she'd been attacked, there should be skin, muscle, and bone as well as clothing."

"These are an unknown species with a potent digestive fluid. The stuff can dissolve anything biological."

" If you don't mind me asking, you are very well informed. Are you a marine biologist or something?"

"Close enough, I guess." Georgia stopped in front of the next door. "Why am I not in shock?" she asked, turning around to face him. "I should be hiding under a table and talking gibberish."

"Shock is what happens after the event, Georgia. Right now, there's too much chemical activity inside to allow you to experience shock. Don't worry, though. I think once this is over, we'll all need to spend a year in therapy." He then rested a knife into the palm of her hand. "Take this," he whispered. "Find somewhere to hide it, and don't let them to know you have it."

"What?"

"They took your weapons. If it happens again, you won't be defenceless."

"Thanks. I think." She concealed the knife under her blouse. "Do you want to do the gun thing again before I open the door?"

Maddock grabbed the handle and pulled. "No need." He held the door open. "After you."

Georgia passed under his arm and moved to the side while the others entered.

"I feel like I've just walked into a pet shop," muttered Alan.

"This one of the resort's aquariums. Don't worry, there's nothing harmful in here." Georgia frowned. The tanks which surrounded the walks were like they always were but the large open tank which ran along the walkway had nothing in it. She approached the tank and peered inside.

"What's wrong?"

She glanced up at Thomas. "This is supposed to be full of Japanese carp."

"Maybe the octopuses got them. They seem to have eaten everything else."

"I guess."

"Unless there's another reason," said Maddock, walking past the pair. He walked between the tanks until he stopped in the middle. "Found it." Maddock placed his hands on top of the tank and leaned a little further. He nodded to himself before quickly returning. "There's a large hole in the bottom of the tank," he said. Georgia, is there another way through?"

She shook her head. "Not that I'm aware of."

"So, the fish escaped," cried Peter. "Does it really matter?" The minion strode down the walkway, dragging his fingers through the water. "The giant octopus is back there. Nothing can get us in here. Back me up here, boss."

Clarence looked reluctant to step in. Even Maddock had moved away from the tank.

"I don't think you should do that," said Maddock. Looking directly at the water.

"Oh, is that right?"

"You think perhaps the carp dug a tunnel? Maybe they found some pickaxes?" He lifted the shotgun.

"So, it's like that? If I don't do as I'm told, you'll shoot me?"

"Get away from there!" Clarence yelled.

Thomas ran over and threw himself on the minion just as the baby Liopleurodon rose out of the water and tried to grab the man's head. Before it could try again, Maddock fired. The noise in the enclosed space almost burst her eardrums, but that was nothing to what the blast did to the animal. The shot reduced its head into a steaming black and crimson lump of meat. The dead creature sank into the water.

"Oh God, oh God! I nearly died. I can't believe I nearly died!" The minion stood up and puffed out his chest. "Yeah, well, that ain't gonna happen. No sea monster is going to eat this guy!" He walked over to the tank and punched the creature's hide.

Georgia saw a stream of bubbles rising to the surface close to the giggling man. She glanced across at Maddock who gave her a slight head shake. The blonde man then forced her to the floor and stood over her when the other one leapt out of the tank and fastened its jaws around the man's shrieking face. Its jaws snapped shut and dropped back into the water before Maddock had time to fire off another shot.

She watched the headless man fall to his knees before his body slapped against the bloodied tiles.

CHAPTER FOURTEEN

Donna White threw herself across the unmade bed and rolled onto the carpet. She scrabbled around looking for something, for *anything*, that might help stop that vile thing from killing her. She reached under the bed and her fingers curled around a wire coat hanger.

Hardly daring to breathe, she shuffled away from the side of the bed, keeping her gaze fixed to the two walls. It had to be in here somewhere. Donna knew for a fact that the octopus wouldn't just go away no matter how much she hoped. It wasn't on the walls or the ceiling. Donna slowly sat up expecting it to jump on her at any moment. She wished her heart would slow down.

Could it have gone? It didn't make any sense; the animal was right behind her. Perhaps her luck was changing for the better after all. She raced across the room and slammed the door shut just in case it decided to come back with some of its friends.

Donna looked at the coat hanger in disbelief. What the hell could she have done with this apart from hang it up in the frigging wardrobe. She pulled the cover off the bed and wrapped it around her wet body. She kinda suspected that her violent shivering was more down to shock than taking that swan through the corridor.

"Clothes," she muttered. "I need dry clothes." Yeah, that would help. Getting warm and dry might ease away some of her mental chaos. Donna doubted it, though. The only thing that could stop her from imploding is the knowledge that she was safe again and away from this place.

She hurried over to the wardrobe and grabbed the door handle just as something black and shiny skittered across the top. Donna yelped and staggered back when the octopus launched its body off the top of the wardrobe. She jumped to the side, scooped up the coat hanger, and cracked the animal as soon as it landed on the bed.

Two of its limbs whipped up and wrapped around her wrist. Donna screamed out in shock. She swung the coat hanger down in a wide arc. The point pierced its gelatinous body at the base and the two tentacles fell off her skin.

"You bastard," she wept. "You utter bastard!" Her sobs quickly turned to hysterical laughter when the cupboard door swung open, and she found herself inundated with a variety of fancy dress costumes. "Oh yeah, because that's normal."

Donna stood up, pulled the coat hanger from the corpse, and wiped it on the mattress. Perhaps it wasn't as useless as she first believed? She checked the rest of the room to make sure that no more of those things had sneaked in. She looked at the mattress. God, how tempting would it be to climb on there, close her eyes, and hope that this was just some stupid nightmare?

No, she dare not do that. This was not safe. There were still loads of those horrible things out there, and she'd already experienced how they reacted when those nightmares caught the scent of their prey.

Her imagination gleefully painted Donna a colourful picture of her opening that door once she'd had her restful sleep. Instead of finding a dozen handsome rescuers out there, hundreds of slimy octopuses would rain down on her.

She wasn't going to allow her stupid mind to make her already desperate situation even worse. No way; not this time. Donna walked over to the door and pulled it wide open. There were no more of those bastard things anywhere in sight, but that didn't mean they weren't out there just waiting for this poor human to venture outside with her trusty coat hanger.

Donna shut the door, walked back to the side of the bed, and sat down. She would leave here, just not yet; not until she'd calmed down and collected her thoughts. Running around in a blind panic was the whole reason why she was in this room in the first place. It was only speed and sheer good luck that had stopped those things from getting her. Donna placed the coat hanger beside her and tried to mentally map out the shortest and quickest route to the main entrance.

Everything went fine until Donna reached the casino where she worked, and then the emotional bubble burst again. She flopped back and watched the ceiling blur under a flood of hot tears. Her life had turned to utter shit the moment she managed to get Gail to work her shift. Back then, the moment that the bubbly girl eagerly nodded to work the shittiest shift in existence, Donna thought that some unknown God had decided to shine down on her. For the first time in months, it looked like her bad luck had changed.

Yeah, right. Donna should have known that there'd be something nasty waiting for her at the end of that glorious rainbow. Nobody liked working the twilight shift as its when all the resident weirdos and the cash-strapped losers crawled out of the woodwork and generally made the casino workers lives miserable. She thought the only reason why Gail agreed is because she was new to the resort and hadn't worked the twilight shift before.

Donna remembered walking out of the staff room with a wide smile fixed to her face, ecstatic at the tantalising prospect of mixing with the resort guests for the first time since she arrived here several months ago. Even the dirty looks her fellow workers gave her as she left the casino failed to put a crimp on her looking forward to her night out.

She sat up and dried her eyes with the bad sheet. Had Gail and the others managed to get out of here okay? They will have done. Donna hadn't seen anyone else since waking up in that stranger's cabin, and she had managed to cover a lot of distance during her panicked dash into this room.

Of all the things that had happened to her since waking up, being unable to remember the face of the man she had slept with last night annoyed her more than anything. It might have been David. She met that one in the Pineapple Club close the main promenade. Tall, handsome, and very rich. Not that the last attribute was all that uncommon on the resort. You needed to have cash to burn to come to this place. Still, it had been a surprise to found a guest who was genuinely easy to talk to.

Thing is, Donna was fairly sure that he'd fallen by the wayside after the third club, meaning she must have woken in the cabin belonging to either Derek or Adam. Like David, they both ticked the heap of money category, but their good looks and charm were sadly lacking. By the time they arrived on the scene, neither of those attributes really mattered thanks to the incredible amount of alcohol that his mates had poured down her neck.

Her invite to Mandy Gilmore's celebratory bash had come as a bit of a surprise to Donna considering she had only known the girl a week. Mandy worked in a rival casino at the other side of the resort, and unlike the crappy joint where Donna worked, the other casino knew how to look after their workers.

Mandy had won the employee of the quarter award, and her prize consisted of a week paid holiday, as well as a single night thank you voucher. Those tickets allowed you and four friends to enjoy the resort's many attractions at no cost. Donna guessed that they'd originally expected the employees to use the voucher to take advantage of the many arcades, parks, and the world-renowned water slides.

Like that was ever going to happen; not when the resort's clubs were overflowing with free booze and millionaire bachelors who knew who to show a pretty girl a good time. There was always the remote chance that the man would sweep them off their feet and whisk them away from this low paid drudgery. It might sound like a remote fantasy, but it could happen.

Donna looked down at the bed sheet trying not to tear up again at the sight of her smudged war paint covering the surface. Perhaps it wasn't that much of a surprise after all. Mandy had chosen her purely for her good looks. She supposed it made sense. Five beautiful girls walking into a club were bound to turn a few heads.

She would never forget the look on plain Gail's face at the thought of earning an extra hundred dollars plus tips. Would Gail have looked so happy if she knew why Donna wanted to swap shifts? It's strange how fate works.

Her mate sure as hell wouldn't have picked Gail to go out with her, so Donnie's plain looking workmate wouldn't have enjoyed the experience of three millionaires plying her with drinks all night while repeating how she looked like a Goddess or some other such nonsense. Then again, Gail wasn't hiding from ravenous invertebrates as big as footballs wanting to eat her face.

The lucky bitch was probably on a rescue boat with all the other survivors, wrapped in blankets, and sipping hot chocolate. Donna stood up. "You had better save me some hot chocolate, because you're not leaving without me."

Before leaving the safety of this room, she would need

something more efficient at killing octopus than a coat hanger. There must be something else in here that would do a better job. As the only thing that could provide an alternative lay inside that wardrobe, Donna hurried over and rifled through all the fancy dress clothing. Her hands came to a dead stop when she found herself staring at a samurai costume complete with a realistic katana. Donna carefully lifted it out of the wardrobe, lifted it above her head, and swung it into the side of the wardrobe. The blade sliced through the thin wood like a hot knife through butter.

"Bloody hell, it's real!"

Maybe her luck had changed for the better after all. Donna pulled the sword out of the wood and laid it on the mattress and looked through the rest of the stuff in case there was anything else interesting.

"You have got to be kidding me," she said, while pulling out a gun from a holster next to a cowboy outfit. It was the real deal, alright, but she couldn't find and ammo for it. Even if Donna had found the ammo, it wouldn't have been much use to her. She'd never fired a gun in her life.

It was best to stick to what she already had. After the terror those bastards had caused her since waking up, getting up close and personal with the slimy bastards sounded like the best idea she'd had all day.

There wasn't anything in there to replace her sodden clothing. Being rescued in her nightwear was bad enough, but they sure as hell were not going to pick her up dressed as Pocahontas! She closed the wardrobe, grabbed the sword, and got ready to face the music.

She pulled open the room door and jumped out, hiding the sword in front of her. There wasn't anything which needed chopping up, so Donna crept along the balcony while gazing at the casino below. It did feel weird being in here where Mandy worked. The layout was the same as her place, but this one didn't feel as grubby. She bet this place never attracted the weirdos. Donna put that down to its placement. This casino was right in the middle of the more exclusive area of the resort. It probably explained why they were more liberal with their employee packages.

The only package Donna craved at this moment was an all-expenses paid package holiday, preferably somewhere hot and dry where there'd be no damn octopuses. The Sahara Desert sounded ideal around about now.

It took her a moment to realise that she was walking in the wrong direction. This was the route Donna took after fleeing from that man's cabin.

It seemed so long ago now, almost a lifetime away when she woke up alone in that luxurious bed, her head resting on deep crimson pillows while a single silk sheet of the same colour covered her naked body. The events of the previous night came to her in broken fragments, but it didn't take a genius to piece together that she'd probably drunk her body weight in booze before allowing some rich dude to take advantage.

She slowly sat up and gazed around the cabin, clocking the two piles of crumpled clothes on the side of the bed. Donna leaned across and picked up the trousers, wincing as a load of loose change toppled out. No matter how hard she tried, she couldn't remember whose bed she'd woken up in. Donna hooked her fingers around the waist band and pulled them tight. Well, he wasn't a porker.

As much as she wanted to stay here, Donna needed to find this mystery guy. Also, her stomach demanded food. She climbed out of the bed, found her underwear, and grabbed a bathrobe which hung from the back of the bedroom door before leaving.

The octopus jumped onto her arm as soon as she opened the bathroom door. Donna screamed while frantically waving her arm about as the animal curled its tentacles around her. She called out for anyone to help her get it off, but her cries went unheeded. In the end, Donna smashed it against the wall, reducing its body into black jellied mush.

She stood there, panting like a warm dog while looking down at the mess on the floor. It took her about a minute to calm herself down before searching through the rest of the apartment looking for her mystery man. He couldn't have left her here. Hell, no; this was his apartment for crying out loud. Unless he'd gone to get them something to eat?

Donna wiped her arm yet again before walking over to the door. It's only when she opened it and saw dozens more of those horrible animals scuttling up and down the walls when she realised something had seriously gone wrong at the resort.

Donna shuddered at the memory of running, screaming, from that apartment and knowing those things were on the walls, ready to leap on her. She gripped the sword even tighter. They weren't going to intimidate her again, that's for damn sure.

Until this moment, she hadn't really given much thought to where her mystery man had disappeared to. Apart from tripping over a pair of black silk shorts outside the apartment door, she hadn't seen a single trace of him during her panicked escape. He wouldn't have left her in there. Perhaps he had gone to look for help, or maybe he was hiding in a closet somewhere? Donna couldn't leave without checking. Hell, he couldn't have gotten that far.

With her mind made up, Donna set off back towards the apartment where she awoke earlier on, deciding to start there first. In her mind, she imagined opening the door to find her mystery man waiting for her. She hurried past a couple of roulette tables, noticing that they looked in better condition than the equipment at her casino, and stopped beside a row of slot machines.

In her mind's eyes, Donna could not remove the image of opening that door and seeing David standing in the middle of that living room floor, that shy smile showing off that set of perfect teeth before running up to her and wrapping those strong arms around Donna's waist.

She walked past the machines, each one promising to make her rich beyond her wildest dreams, and resisted the urge to smash them all to pieces. Donna had to stop at the last machine and grab the Perspex front to stop herself from falling. All the strength in her legs had just left her. Donna angrily wiped her eyes. "Thank you, body," she snarled. "Thank you very much."

Donna was going into shock.

Sliding down the front of the machine and having a bit of a rest on that nice thick carpet sounded like the best idea that she'd had in ages. Donna managed to keep hold of her sword while bringing her knees up to her chest. God, she was cold all of a sudden. Perhaps leaving all that fancy dress clothing in that cupboard wasn't such a good idea after all? She might have looked like a bit of a prat, but at least she wouldn't be shivering.

David would look fantastic dressed up as a Japanese samurai. Donna allowed her eyes to drop while she imagined her dream man slowly peeling off the armour while murmuring sweet nothings in her eye. She could almost hear those honey-covered words too!

She snapped open her eyes. Oh God, it was no fantasy; that was his voice. Only they were not soothing calm words. Donna got to her knees just as three figures were pushed past the open casino entrance doors. One of them was definitely David, still dressed in the expensive casual suit she remembered. Only now, it looked far worse for wear just like the owner.

One of the figures, a sobbing, brown haired middle-aged woman, collapsed. Two other men rushed to her. They both wore what looked like police riot gear. What the hell was this? Instead of helping her up, the two men started booting the poor woman. They only paused when David rushed back and attempted to help the woman back onto her feet. When the men restarted their assault, David savagely pushed one of the armoured men back who tripped up over his own feet, and fell against the wall. The remaining man responded by taking a pistol out of a holster and pressing the muzzle against David's forehead.

"Oh, Jesus!" she gasped.

There was a loud pop, and David flew backwards. Donna stared in disbelief at the patch of red and grey fluid now dripping down the wall where David once stood. "You bastards! You evil bastards!"

The men turned her way. Donna saw them raise their weapons; she moaned in terror before spinning around and stumbling forward. She heard two more loud pops, and the slot machine above her exploded, showering her head and shoulders with pieces of glass.

She managed to get to her feet and raced through the casino, listening to the two men running a after her. Donna barged through a set of staff only doors. She had two choices, either up or down. Her choice was made up for her at the sight of a small black octopus clinging to the wall above her. Donna ran down the steps, praying that the octopus and any of its hidden mates would dive on those two murdering bastards as soon as they entered the stairwell.

Donna reached the next level by the time the two men pushed through the doors above her. She placed her hands flat against the surface and listened to the mechanical sound of their indecipherable conversation while she hardly daring to breathe. Donna heard another loud pop followed by a sharp laugh. So much for the octopus attacking them.

One of them ran up the stairs, leaving the remaining man stood directly above her. What was he doing? The tips of Donna 's fingers traced the gap between the doors. She could hear him tapping his nails against the wood. Donna silently counted to three then slowly pulled the door open wide enough to slip her body through. She eased it shut then ran through a storeroom full of brown cardboard boxes stacked from floor to ceiling against two of the walls. It became totally clear as soon as soon as she reached the end wall why that man hadn't followed her. There was no point. She'd trapped herself. The bastard with that gun now stood between Donna and her freedom.

This couldn't be the end, no way, not after all the shit she'd just gone through. There had to be another way out of here! Donna looked at the floor and nodded in relief when she noticed one of the boxes at the end of the room was damp. She ran over, grabbed the box, and slid it towards her.

"Got you!" She'd uncovered a grate large enough for her to fit down. Donna dropped to her knees, lifted up the cover, and stared into its clear blue depths. The water lapped over the edges and trickled across the tiles. She would have to hold her breath and hope to Christ that there would be fresh air at the other end.

The sound of running feet removed her last bit of trepidation. Donna jumped into the water and swam as fast as she could towards the light a few metres in front of her. She almost breathed in a lungful of cold Atlantic Ocean when something brushed passed her legs. Donna tilted her head downwards. It looked a bit like a capsized boat. The realisation came far too late for Donna White when the 'boat' lifted its huge head and lunged for her legs.

She twisted her body then rolled backwards before trying to swim back to that grate. She even managed to touch the edges with her fingertips before a sudden blast of searing agony crashed into her body as the monster's teeth sliced through Donna's mid-section.

Seconds before her life expired, the woman remembered the face of the man who had kissed her the night before. It was Adam.

CHAPTER FIFTEEN

Maddock kicked another empty shell case and watched it roll across the black and white tiled kitchen floor and disappear under a cupboard unit. He approached the dining table and leaned against the back of one of the three chairs that was arranged around the table. A rough line of cratered holes ran across the middle of the wall in front of him. In fact, everywhere he looked in this small kitchen Maddock saw evidence of gunfire.

"Anything in there to eat?"

He turned his head and looked through the remains of the smashed door and saw Georgia smiling at him. Thomas stood behind her with his back turned, watching Ryan and Clarence. "I haven't looked yet," he replied.

What could have happened in here? Apart from the empty shells cases scattered across the floor and the holes in the walls, he found no body or blood. It looked as though a number of people had barricaded themselves in here. Possibly two people from the number of cups on the table. Splintered pieces of the remaining chairs, a bookcase, and a moveable wall unit from the next room covered the floor in front of the door. They obviously weren't hiding from the sea monster and he didn't think the octopuses had done all this damage either.

Once again, Maddock found himself filling up his head with even more questions that he couldn't answer. If he had his way, they wouldn't have stopped at all but, of course, the decision to keep going was taken out of his hands by Georgia who told him that she needed to eat.

As soon as food was mentioned, Maddock realised that he couldn't actually remember the last time he put something in his stomach. Even so, it still felt like madness to stop for anything, even food.

He opened one of the cupboards above sink. He found a packet of chocolate cookies, two tins of hot dogs, and a tin of meatballs. Maddock brought his collection over to the table and dropped the stuff in the middle.

"Help yourself," he said, as they filed inside. Maddock took a couple of the cookies from the packet before walking through the devastated door. He made his way over to the apartment door and opened it a crack. An unfamiliar melody drifted up from one of the deserted shopping malls below them. It's all he could hear.

Well, that and the quiet murmurs coming from behind him.

"How are you holding up?"

Maddock turned around. "Should I not be saying that to you, Georgia?"

She placed her fingers around his hand. "Probably. Truth is, even if you did ask me, I'm not sure that I'd be able to give you a straight answer. I mean, even after everything that we've been through, I still keep asking myself if this is real at all. How stupid is that?"

Her fingers were so warm. Maddock turned his wrist around, opened is fingers, and closed his hand around hers. "It isn't stupid at all, Georgia. What you're doing is perfectly normal. Believe me. I was trained for this, and this is taking its toll on me too."

"You were trained to fight giant octopuses," she replied.

"Funny. No, I mean I was trained to be able to react during high stress fluid situations. I think the shit storm that we're all currently in falls straight in that category." He nodded over at the three men sitting around the table. Not only do I have your safety in mind, I have to ensure our two new friends behave."

"What's that?"

He spun back to the open door. Crawling up the front of a shop window, Maddock saw one of the smaller octopuses. It stopped halfway up then abruptly turned to the side. "That's unbelievable," he gasped when the animal literally ran across the side of the glass and vanished around the corner. "I've never seen one move so fast before! Do you think something spooked it?"

Her hand violently shook. Maddock looked down at her bulging eyes then followed her gaze over towards a shop doorway a few metres to the left of where he saw the octopus.

"Shit!" he hissed. A thick black tentacle had just pushed up through one of the grates in the middle of the floor. It felt around the perimeter of the grate for a couple of seconds. It reminded

Maddock of some weird alien periscope. Judging from how fast that little octopus moved, perhaps he wasn't that far of the mark. It then sank back below the floor. He almost expected it to slide the cover back over the grate.

He shut the door. "We need to get out of here."

"If we can," she replied.

"What do you mean?"

"You know exactly what I mean, Maddock. Just look at the state of that kitchen. Do you really believe that the people who'd barricaded themselves in there were hiding from the octopuses? Come on, man. Just say it. The animals aren't the real danger here. Maddock, this place is a fish tank, and we're the food flakes. We don't stand a chance!"

He roughly grabbed her shoulders and pushed her back out of sight of the others. "Stop that; stop it right now."

"But..."

"There's no buts," hissed Maddock. "Just listen. Don't you think we've all wondered what is going on here? Course we have, but you know what? It doesn't change a thing, and it doesn't change what we all have to do. For you, Georgia, that means you guide us out of this rabbit warren. Do you understand? Focus on the mission; it's that simple." Maddock let her go and walked back over to the door. "You were going to suggest that we all stay here and weather the storm."

"How did you know?"

"You haven't eaten anything for a start. It obvious that you haven't thought this through. Even if the others agreed to batten down the hatches, which they wouldn't, are you comfortable with two convicted murderers? Three, if you include me."

She shook her head. "Maybe not."

He walked back into the kitchen and pulled a tin of half eaten hot dogs out of Ryan 's hand. "Time to saddle up, guys. Rest period is over." Maddock gave the tin to Georgia. "Here you go. Get them down your neck. We've lost enough time already."

She plucked a sausage out of the tin. "What's your role then, Maddock?"

"To keep you safe," he replied. "Without you, we'll be going around in circles until someone or something pick us off. Before we do leave, I do have one question. Where the frig did that monster come from?"

I could tell you, but I'm not sure you'll like the answer."

"Christ. Just spill it, Georgia. It's not like it'll make our situation any worse than it is now."

"Fair enough. It's simple really. The huge ones were the same size as all the smaller ones not so long ago. Once the human food supply had gone, they turned on each other. The stronger animals ate the weaker ones."

"Nothing can get to that size in just a few hours. It's impossible!"

Georgia smiled tightly. "I said you wouldn't like the answer."

Maddock looked over at Thomas. "How are our two pals doing?"

"They're behaving," he replied, grinning.

"Then I think we'd better get moving." Maddock picked up the shotgun and opened the door. He stared at that open grate for a few seconds before stepping out onto the balcony. "Wait here." Maddock ran down the stairs, crossed over to that cover, and carefully slid it back into place with his foot. He signalled for the others to join him.

"Okay, Georgia," he whispered. "The floor is all yours. Lead the way."

She looked back at that grate before hurrying past the shop front. Maddock took up position directly behind the woman and fell into step. The two other prisoners were behind him. Georgia didn't look back once as she made her way along the deserted promenade. It looked like every shop here was deserted, although Maddock wasn't entirely sure that some of them were as empty as they appeared. He kept glimpsing shadows which quickly darted out of sight when their group moved walked past. Those shadows could have just been a figment of his imagination, or they might even belong to some stray human. Hell, it could have been a lone octopus; it didn't matter anymore. This place now belonged to the monstrous behemoths, and both land and water had now become as dangerous as each other.

Maddock's gaze landed on every grate the group walked past, expecting the cover to fly off at any moment before a tentacle rose up and took another one down into the cold depths of the ocean. He imagined himself standing in front of the cowering woman, blasting away at the monster until he ran out of shells, or the kraken ran out of tentacles. Maddock spun around and looked back to where he'd seen that thick tentacle. "Georgia. Stop a moment." The three other men looked at him. Thomas appeared concerned while the others both sneered at Maddock.

"What's wrong?"

"Do you think there's more than one of those huge octopuses?"

"I think so. Why do you ask?"

"This resort is pretty big, isn't it? So, what are the chances of seeing it again so soon?"

"You think it's following us?" asked Thomas."

Maddock nodded. "It could be under us right now."

"Or you could be just trying to scare us all witless," replied Clarence. He turned to Georgia. "Madam, would you be so kind to tell us how close we are to our destination?"

"Not far now, I guess. Once we leave this shopping district, there's an emergency exit which will take us through some of the maintenance areas. From there, we go down one short corridor, and we'll be at the casting off station. Five minutes tops, I'd say."

Clarence grinned. "Thank you, Georgia. I'm so grateful for your blind honesty." He looked sharply at Ryan. "Now."

Before Maddock could react, the other prisoner rushed Georgia, wrapped his arm around her neck, and pushed the muzzle of a pistol against her temple. Clarence walked past Maddock and snatched the shotgun out of his hands.

"I'll take that, if you don't mind." He looked across at Thomas. "Drop the toy pistol, or I'll drop you." He ran his fingers across the stock. "Very pretty; much prettier than the pistol I found under the table in that apartment." He grinned. "Still, I don't think Ryan is all that bothered."

"Stop this, Clarence, for crying out loud. "We need to stick together if we're all going to get out of here alive."

"No, you're wrong there, Maddock." He ran past Ryan and the sobbing woman. "As you have treated us with some dignity, I won't kill you. That will change if you try to follow us. Don't worry about your woman, Maddock. As soon as we're safe, I promise that I'll let her go. You can trust me on this."

Maddock clenched his fists in anger and frustration as the prisoners dragged Georgia away. He waited until they were out of sight before retrieving the dart gun. He placed it back in the guard's hand.

"What are we going to do now?"

"We go after them," he growled. "What else can we do?" Maddock patted the man on the shoulders before racing along the promenade. He made it to the end, just in time to see a door across from where they stood swing shut.

As he ran towards that door, all Maddock could think about was that he'd failed the one task he had set himself.

"Here," said Thomas, pushing the gun into his hands. "You're a better shot than I am." He took the gun without saying a word. He dare not trust his mouth. Christ, what a mess. Thomas only had one job. How could he not notice one of those clowns picking up that gun? The guards know how quick the prisoners are at snatching stuff and hiding them.

He slammed the grey bar down, pushed open the door, and dived through the opening. Coming up from a roll, Maddock found himself standing on another gantry which encircled the dark room. He saw two flights of steps, leading down to the next level. One flight a few paces to his left and the other set of steps opposite him.

There was no sign of their quarry. Maddock leaned over the railing and groaned in despair. Water had flooded the floor below and was rising fast. If they didn't move, the only other way out would be underwater!

Thomas grabbed him. "Move it, Maddock!" The guard ran over to the stairs and jumped into the water. Maddock ran after him. He climbed down a couple of steps before following Thomas into the water. It had reached his shoulders already. Thomas was almost at the door when they both turned around at the sound of a colossal smash coming from the other side of the room.

"Oh, fuck!" gasped Maddock. "Please not that again." The door beside Thomas wasn't the only way in here. The room opened up into a large hall. Maddock backed away, watching in total terror at the sight of the huge reptilian sea monster swimming straight at them. "Get that door open!"

"I can't," cried Thomas. "It's locked."

"Oh, Christ. We're dead."

The Beast slowed down. It opened its cavernous mouth before continuing to approach their position. Maddock had pressed his back against Thomas. He aimed the dart gun at the animal, determined not to go down without a fight.

Maddock aimed at its huge black eye and paused.

"What are you doing, man?" screamed Thomas. "Shoot the bastard!"

He couldn't do anything, Maddock couldn't even move. His attention was too focussed on the figure wading along side the monster, totally calm while patting the creature's flank as he approached them.

"I don't believe this. Prowler?"

The man nodded. "Indeed. It's been a bit of a weird day, don't you think?" He stopped in between the creature and them. "You'd better follow me. I have something to show you."

CHAPTER SIXTEEN

The gun shop had not tempted him inside despite the varied selection of unbelievably expensive weapons displayed in the shop window. The Prowler hadn't even taken a handgun. The contents of the shop next door had the been the sole reason for his diversion. The thermal waterproof trousers in that specialist shop were so worth the trek back through the resort and onto the promenade. It had to be the best decision he'd made all day. It even topped stringing that man up to feed his new pets. The joy he had felt when that magnificent beast's teeth sank into his flesh did feel so good, but these trousers gave him lasting satisfaction. To his mindset, that was so much more important.

If that guard hadn't been here, The Prowler might have even shared this insight with Maddock and point to their own sodden clothing as an example of not being appropriately dressed for the situation. The Prowler kept his thoughts to himself. He wasn't going to say shit to a screw. If the shoe had been on the other foot, that gun shop would now be standing empty, and these two chattering monkeys would have shot this place to hell while dressed like Rambo.

Even with their single gun, Maddock and the guard had done okay. Not bad considering their inability to cohabit the resort with the new owners. The Prowler knew of Maddock's military history, so no doubt that would have come in handy. Saying that, considering that amount of noise they were generating they hadn't learnt that much. Still, he was happy that he'd not been eaten as he really did like Maddock. Unlike the others, the guy had treated him like a proper human being.

He brought them out of the cold water and slowed down to wipe the top of his waterproofs. The gesture was more to annoy the guard than to dry his clothing. He wondered if he would have been so frivolous with his time if he knew what was at stake? It probably wouldn't have made that much difference.

The Prowler stopped. The time difference did mean that these two were still alive; that counted for something. He wouldn't have these two chattering idiots on the monitors running after the other undesirables. If he hadn't raced to help them, these two wouldn't have lasted more than a few seconds. Maddock's popgun would have only annoyed the animal.

"How the hell did you manage that?"

Should it surprise him that the screw hadn't thanked him for saving his life? Probably not. The Prowler had expected that response. Still, the man's apparent disregard for his self-sacrifice did ground his gears no matter how hard The Prowler tried to suppress it.

"Thanks for showing up when you did, buddy," said Maddock. "That's two I owe you."

He muttered a no problem. At least one of them had the common decency to acknowledge his importance. The Prowler wasn't going to allow that screw to get to him. There was too much at risk to let emotions blind him.

They were almost back at his base of operations. With their help, he should be able to achieve his objective in no time. Once they understood the gravity of their situation his attitude was bound to alter. Even the guard couldn't be that cold hearted.

"Come on, man. Tell me. How the hell did you stop that bloody monster from eating us?" Thomas ran his hand down his face. "I've never seen anything like that before."

"Fine, keep it to yourself. I'm just glad that you stopped that bloody monster from eating us." "I've never seen anything like that before." He looked past The Prowler. "I hope you know where you're going." Thomas glanced at Maddock. "Look, we were with a girl we'd found. We need to get back to her."

"Yeah, I saw her with you two," he replied. "I shouldn't worry too much about that one. The Beast won't hurt her; not yet, anyway." The Prowler decided that Thomas should be satisfied with that explanation. "Right, come on. We've wasted enough time as it is. It's isn't far now."

"Have you lost all your senses?" he snarled. Thomas strode up to The Prowler. "It wasn't a request, prisoner. There's no multiple-choice answers. You're going to take us to Georgia, or you won't survive the consequences."

"Oh, did I mention that we need to be quiet around now?" he replied, totally ignoring the insignificant little man's threat.

"Don't you tell me what to do."

Maddock hadn't said a single word during this altercation, although his body language suggested that not everything was peachy between these two. That wasn't shocking. After all, once a screw always a screw. "Are you going to stop talking?"

The man's face screwed up in fury. He sensed the fist before Thomas threw it and managed to dive to the left. The blow only glanced the side of The Prowler's face; it still hurt like hell, though. There was no follow through as Maddock pulled Thomas back and ordered the screw to calm down. The Prowler reluctantly put the knife back inside his jacket pocket.

"We can't leave her with those animals, man. Surely you can see that?"

"I know, and believe me, I hate this, too, but we're in a state of war." The Prowler sighed. "Maddock. Believe me. As soon as we're done, we'll all go and rescue her. I am right about those two, you know. They will not harm a hair on her head, at least not until they're out of here. She's too useful."

"Not good enough." Thomas snatched the gun off Maddock and aimed it at The Prowler. "No more games. Do as you're told or die."

The prowler gave the man his best submissive face. He even dropped his shoulders. "You had better follow me." He carried on walking then took a sharp right. He picked up his pace knowing that the screw was right behind him. After a couple of minutes, The Prowler slowed down, knowing from the subtle change in aroma that he was close to them. It was time to make his persecutor angry. That shouldn't pose much of a problem. He slowed down then stopped before turning around. He waited for the screw to reach him before he placed his hands on his hips. They were so close now.

"There's been people like you ordering me about all my life," he hissed. "Thinking you know better when really you don't have a clue." He glanced over at Maddock and hoped he wouldn't interfere this time. He so didn't want him to get hurt. The Prowler took out his knife and waved it in front of his face. He dare not speak now. It had become way too dangerous. He knew they were here; the moving shadows on the wall just behind the screw confirmed this.

"What, you threatening me now? With a knife?? he yelled. "I don't believe this. Good God, just how dumb can anyone be?"

The guard's fury transformed to terror when the grate between the two men slid to the side and a shiny, black tentacle rushed out from the darkness and curled around Thomas's ankles. He screamed out, begging for help, when another limb rose up and waved menacingly from side to side. The monster tugged once, and Thomas fell to the floor. It dragged the shrieking man towards the small hole. The Prowler saw Maddock trying to reach for the fallen gun but he simply shook his head and motioned the man to keep his distance.

The other tentacle took the man's other ankle and pulled his legs into the hole. The Prowler edged along the wall, scooping up the gun as he passed the guard. The man's screams had now become low moans of agony. The Prowler guessed that was probably due to the monster trying to squeeze the man through a hole half his size.

"Oh, my God!" Maddock switched his horrified gaze from the dying man and glared at The Prowler. "Did you know this was going to happen?" He looked at the gun that The Prowler was now pointing at Maddock's mid-section. "You did! Oh, hell, why, man?"

"He was a threat to me." The Prowler listened to the dying man's last squealing alongside the sound of cracking and splintering as that behemoth finally pulled his arms and shoulders through that hole. "If you want to be next then fine. You stay here." The Prowler handed the gun back to Maddock. "I'd rather you didn't. I need your help."

He turned around and hurried back towards his original destination, confident that Maddock would make the right decision. He had now seen first-hand the evil which infested this place and would want to do anything in his power to help The Prowler stop it from spreading.

It took him just minutes to get back on the right track. His sense of direction was second to none. The Prowler had studied the available maps. It was impossible for him to get lost. He stopped at the end of a plain cream corridor, dropped to his knees, and pushed his hands against the side of the wall to his left. A small panel clicked and slid back to reveal two silver buttons on top of each other. "Just where they were supposed to be," he muttered. The Prowler turned his head. "Obviously, they had remotes, but I couldn't find any which worked. I guess the power outage this place suffered before the system crashed must have fried the circuits. Not to worry; the designers built in these back-ups at every entry point, and I know these work." He motioned him to come closer. "Don't worry, I won't bite." The Prowler attempted to smile but gave that up as a bad job when Maddock backed away. "It's an elevator, Maddock. That's all."

He pressed the button at the top then stood up. The sound of hidden machinery broke the uncomfortable silence.

"This is no trick?"

Before The Prowler could tell Maddock to stop acting like a child, the man jumped onto the rising floor panel. He grinned. "Get ready to enter wonderland, Alice."

The ceiling slowly slid open. He wondered what must be going through Maddock's mind right about now. Was this as exciting to him as it was to The Prowler when he first discovered the sole purpose of this resort? The man didn't look all that impressed. He hoped Maddock still wasn't thinking about that guard's unfortunate death. The Prowler wanted to tell his colleague that the guard brought it on himself. If he'd listened then Thomas would still be alive.

Once the floor panel clicked into place. The Prowler knew exactly what he should do first. He ran over to the monitor banks and flicked through the channels relating to the relevant section. "There you are," he said. "Maddock, stop staring, and come over here. Hurry up!"

The man turned and strode over. "This had better be good."

He stabbed his finger at one of the nine monitors which displayed sections of the west side of the resort. "You see? What did I tell you? The girl is alive and well. Just like I predicted." To be honest, The Prowler wasn't totally sure that she would still be breathing. He, as well as everybody else, knew of Ryan's past. Perhaps if The Beast hadn't been there, then the situation could have been a lot different. He watched relief flooding Maddock's face and realised that he had misjudged the situation. This man here would have killed The Prowler stone dead if that monitor screen had showed the girl's violated corpse instead of the two men walking a couple of footsteps behind the woman.

"Where are they? More to the point, how long will it take us to get there?"

"Calm your jets, Maddock. Like I said, she's safe right now. I promise I'll get you to her. I just need your help first." He quickly turned and danced his fingers over the control panel, bringing up what he considered vital images to help convince the man to stay. "Look, just look at this." He pointed to the monitor on the bottom right which showed a black, stubby craft sitting on the ocean bed. "That thing and the people who run it are the ones that are responsible for all this mess, Maddock. It opened up a cavern that's been sealed for millions of years. Thing is, the bastards knew about the octopuses. As for the Liopleurodon pair, I'm not sure. They kept the octopus population low and stopped them from getting out of control. It was the perfect micro-bio system."

"Great. Thanks for the lesson, professor. I feel so educated. Now stop fucking about and tell me where the girl is!"

"Maddock, you need to listen to me. Most of the octopus are here in the resort grouped together. That won't last. They'll soon move out into the ocean, and when that happens, you can say goodbye to your smoked kippers as well as everything else which moves below the ocean. You've seen how fast those vile creatures have grown. If we don't stop them while most of them are contained, this planet is doomed."

Maddock turned from the monitor screens, found a computer chair nearby, and slumped in it. "For crying out loud, man. Look I admire your devotion towards the animals, I really do, but don't you think you're overreacting here? The best thing we can do is get out while we still can, and let the authorities deal with it."

The Prowler expected more from Maddock. Of all people, he thought that this man would at least listen. He went through his earlier conversations and wondered whether perhaps he could be the one at fault here. What if he was the one at fault, and the reason why Maddock wasn't panicking was because he hadn't made himself clearer? That did sound plausible. He'd never been all too great in communicating his thoughts to other humans.

"Maddock. The authorities won't be coming." He paused for dramatic effect. "The authorities won't be coming because they already know. This is no holiday resort. It's a military research installation. The resort was just a cover." His lone audience sat captivated. The Prowler tried not to punch the air in triumph. Instead, he pressed home his advantage. "Maddock. Do you remember seeing those pretend towns that the US military built in the middle of the desert back in the 50s?"

Maddock nodded.

"They used to test their nuclear bombs. We'll, that's what *this* is. It's a testing zone." He walked over to the man and gently pulled Maddock back to the monitors. "They believed they could use this new species of octopus as a bioweapon. It's understandable. They are highly aggressive, bloody hard to kill, and are equally at home in water or on land. Only they were running out of specimens. My guess is that a few of them had found a way out of their natural home and were picked up by someone associated with the military who saw their potential." He changed the views on three of the cameras then stepped back to allow Maddock an unrestricted view of the nightmares currently travelling through the resort corridors.

"Oh, my God. Look at the size of them! The bastards are even bigger."

The Prowler suppressed a shudder. They had compressed their bodies in order to squeeze inside a two-metre-wide corridor. Four limbs were in front, and the remaining four trailed behind. It was their speed which scared him the most. They'd be able to run down anything slower than a large dog.

"I have no idea how big they're going to get. Twice, three times the size?" He shrugged. "Even at that size, there isn't any animal living which wouldn't end up as food. Remember, these things have reached that size in about a day."

"A bioweapon?"

He nodded. "From what I can work out, they were trying to insert a genetic strand which would kill them after a few hours.

Only it wasn't working on the few specimens they managed to find. They needed more; hence the drilling. Looks like they didn't realise how many there were trapped down there."

"Okay, I believe you. They're a menace, but what can we do about it?"

"I'll admit, I had hoped that the Liopleurodons would sort out the problem, but there were just too many even for those. Also, they separated so the female could give birth." The Prowler chuckled. "So, you want to what we can do about it. Take a look at this, Maddock." He activated a couple more cameras. Two more monitors changed to show a cream coloured room full of a dozen metal coffin shaped cubicles with thick, ribbed tubing connecting them together."

"What am I looking at here?"

"This, my friend, is the resort's beating heart. A highly experimental fusion generator."

He shook his head. "No. No way. There's no such thing."

"Next you'll be telling me that giant octopus of prehistoric sea monsters don't exist either." He pressed a couple more buttons on the control panel, and one of the cameras zoomed in to one of the metal cubicles. "Take a look at that, Maddock."

He leaned closer. "They're explosives."

"Thermal charges to be precise. As they are, if I detonated them, they'd make a hell of a mess, but not enough to cause a meltdown. To do that, we need to switch them off." He reached into his pocket and brought out two large keys. "I can't do this alone. The two cut-off panels are on the opposite end of this room, and they need turning simultaneously. Once shut off, the detonations will vaporise this place and everything in it. Goodbye threat." He passed Maddock one of the keys. "Come on, time is wasting."

"Wait, stop. What about Georgia?"

The Prowler smiled. "We'll meet up with them near the reactor. You can deal with The Beast and his lapdog then we can all get out of here together." He walked over to the first shut-off panel and inserted the key. "Are you ready?"

"How can you possibly know where they're going?"

I have the keys to the castle, Maddock. I've been locking doors and opening them in order to direct them to where I want them to go." He grinned. "Now, if you've finished gobbing off, can we get on with it?"

The Prowler waited for Maddock to push his key into hole. He gave one nod then turned it to the side. A girl's voice announced a warning stating the facility is powering down. "Right, let's get moving!" He hurried over to the floor panel and waited for his new companion to catch up. "I want to hurt The Beast, Maddock. Will you let me hurt him before we leave?"

"Fine, sure. Let's just get a move on."

The Prowler pressed the button to activate the elevator. As the motors whined, he couldn't help but grin. For once, everything was falling into place. Nothing could go wrong. The floor below slowly came into view. The Prowler turned around. "Maddock, don't look so worried. It's almost over."

The man stumbled back, almost falling off the platform.

"Stop it, you're making me edgy now." He then saw the shadow of a thick tentacle creeping past his legs, a split second before it wrapped around his thighs. "Oh God, Maddock!" he wailed. "Help me."

The man raised the gun, pointed the muzzle directly at The Prowler's forehead. The last thing he saw was Maddock's finger tightening on the trigger.

CHAPTER SEVENTEEN

She knew that one of those things was close by. By now, Georgia had come to recognise the cloying aroma that the krakens gave off. Unfortunately, she had put her damn foot in her mouth earlier on and explained the reason for the smell to Laurel and Hardy.

Why the hell did she have to open her gob? If she'd not said anything, there's a good chance that at least one of them would be octopus food by now. Georgia stopped beside the next door and placed her hand on the top of the lever, only for Ryan to wrap his arms around her waist and squeeze.

"Not so fast, little lady," he whispered in her ear.

She jerked her head to the side when he flicked out his tongue and ran it over her lobe. Georgia pushed her fingernails into his wrist, receiving a tighter squeeze, and a quiet chuckle for her efforts. He pulled her out of the way to allow the other man to check the door.

"Locked," he muttered. Clarence winked at Georgia then motioned Ryan to let her go before he pointed at the next door further up the corridor.

Ryan removed his arms, performed a clumsy bow then brought his wrist up to his face. He turned it around to show the damage she'd caused. Two crescent shaped holes had already filled up with blood. Ryan turned the wrist back and lapped up the blood without taking his eyes off her. He only stopped when Clarence gave him a soft kick.

Her eyes darted to the end of this corridor. Surely one of these doors must be open. It would take her just seconds to run to that farthest door and get the hell away from these two bastards. Georgia looked back to Clarence to discover his gun had appeared out of nowhere and was now pointing straight at her forehead. Oh, God, how did he do that?

The man waved the end of his gun up and down with that smug smile plastered across his greasy fat face. What the hell was wrong with her? A loud scream would easily wipe that smile away. Oh, yeah, that'd do alright. Scream and shout, make as much noise as she could, and then stand back while the krakens grabbed these two jokers and turned them into meat soup.

Ryan slammed the base of his palm between her shoulder blades causing her to drop to her knees. He reached down and dragged her back up. "No lying down on the job, pretty lady." He pinched her backside. "Not yet, anyway. Not until we're safe."

She pushed him away and strode towards the next door, angry and ashamed with herself for not being strong enough to do what she knew was the right thing to do. Oh, Christ, these guys were violent escaped felons; neither of them were going to let her go once she'd taken them to the port. They had made that perfectly clear. So why hadn't she started screaming? Georgia wasn't going to last long anyway. Surely it was better to die in defiance rather than go out after these vile animals had finished playing with her.

Georgia almost did scream out when she found out that the next door was unlocked. Both Ryan and Clarence were on her before she had time to make her break for freedom.

The big man covered her mouth and bundled her inside. "Leave the door open, Ryan, and get behind it."

"What for?"

"There's someone coming, that's what for. Now do as you're told!"

The fat man dragged her back through a cream coloured room full of large metal containers. His hand stayed in place denying her the chance to look for any other exit. All she saw was the other thug taking up position behind that door.

"If I get just one peep out of you, bitch, you'll find out what agony really means." To emphasise his point, Clarence planted his thick fingers on her inner thigh and squeezed.

The pain shot up her leg and exploded inside her head. He had clamped his hand even tighter against her mouth to stop her from crying out.

She swallowed hard at the sight of a figure framed in the doorway. Even through her tear-blurred vision, Georgia knew that Maddock had found them! A sharp jab to the side warned her about trying anything funny. Like that could possibly happen. This man had practically immobilised her.

"Thank God it's you, Maddock. Can you help me out here? This one was bitten by one of those octopus things. I think it's poisoned her."

"Where's Ryan?"

Was he really believing this bullshit? She squirmed, trying to free more of her body, but it was useless. Georgia wasn't going anywhere.

"Hurry up, man. Can't you see that she's fitting?"

Maddock then did the one thing that Georgia had never expected. He laughed.

"Yeah, sure she is. Clarence, you're such a dickhead." His gaze then switched to her. "I'm sorry, Georgia. I can't take you with me. No hard feelings." Maddock gave them a mock salute before slamming the door shut.

Ryan came out from behind the door. "What a piece of shit!" he snarled. "I hope he gets eaten." Ryan then smiled at Georgia. "I bet you must be gutted, Princess. There's no hero coming to rescue you."

Clarence loosened his grip. "Well, that was unexpected."

She wrestled herself off the man. Unexpected? Oh, God. The bastard had just signed her death sentence. These two were going to... Her thought stayed unfinished as Maddock burst through the door and shot Ryan in the ankle. When he didn't go down, Maddock shot out his other ankle.

Clarence reach out and dragged her back towards him. He wrapped his arm around her neck. "Put that down, or I swear to God that I'll break her neck!" Clarence tightened his grip. "Do as you're told, Maddock. You know I'll do it."

Maddock lowered the gun.

"There's a good boy. Now drop it, and kick the gun over."

Instead of obeying him, Maddock crouched. "Georgia, honey. Do you the remember the present I gave you? Well this is the time to use it."

Oh God! How could she have forgotten about that? Georgia reached into her pocket, pulled out the little blade, and slammed it into the man's guts then twisted it. He let out a squeal before staggering back. Clarence tripped up over his own feet and crashed to the floor. Georgia jumped on his stomach and lifted the knife, intending to stick this through his eye and into his brain. Maddock grabbed her arm as she brought it down.

"I have a much better idea." Maddock picked up the gun that Ryan had dropped. "Watch this." He gave her the gun then stood next to the groaning man's feet. "A quick death is too good for you," he said. Maddock lifted his leg and slammed it down on Clarence's ankle."

The cracking of his bone was audible over Ryan's sobbing. She watched him run over to the metal coffin at the back of the room. "What are you doing?"

"Setting the timer," he replied. Maddock ran back over to her and took Georgia in his arms. "I can't tell you how happy I am to see you're okay." He wrapped his hand around hers then gently walked her over to the door.

"What timer?"

Maddock turned and grinned at Ryan. "How's the legs? I guess walking for you is going to be a bit of a problem." He winked at Georgia. "Thing is, this facility is nuclear powered, and we're all in the reaction chamber." He pointed to a small rectangular object stuck to that metal coffin. "That over there is a thermal charge." He grabbed the door handle. "Have a nice life - all ten minutes of it." He closed the door, muffling their insults and begging.

"We need to move it," he said.

"I don't even know where we are anymore, Maddock. I'm totally lost. Also, most of the doors are locked," she cried.

"No problem there," replied Maddock. He pulled out a handheld device a bit larger than a cell phone. "I picked this up earlier." Maddock showed her the screen which displayed a map above a virtual keypad. He tapped the map a couple of times then typed a sequence on the keypad. A thin red line appeared on the map. "All the doors are now unlocked, and that's our route out." He grinned. "Hope you can keep up!"

What was wrong with the man? He was treating this like some kind of school sports day. Maddock was already at the far end of the corridor and waving her on. Georgia gave the door and the muffled shouting the bird before racing after him.

"Just how are we going to get out of here and far enough away to avoid being boiled alive in just ten minutes?"

He pushed her through the open door then guided her into what looked like a small auditorium. It took a moment to recognise this place. Georgia had been here a couple of times on her days off to watch the free movies. What the hell? She turned back to find the door they'd just come through blended into the wall.

"Come on, not far to go now."

"Maddock, please. Will you answer me?"

The man spun around, grabbed both her shoulders and leaned closer. "I've been wanting to do this for quite some time." Maddock gently kissed her."

When he broke off, Georgia thought she saw a glimpse of his true feelings hiding behind this thin veneer of false exuberance. Maddock was just as terrified as she was.

"I lied to them, Georgia. The next few minutes are going to be pure hell for those bastards," he snarled. "They're not going to stop shouting and screaming. With luck, the krakens will find a way to open that door before everything is vaporised." Maddock led her through another hidden door behind the movie screen. "There we go," he said, smiling. "Our way out of here."

Georgia felt the breath go out of her at the sight of three submersibles stationed at the far end of the underground docks. She looked fearfully at Maddock. "Now what do we do?" Over twenty small octopuses lay between them and their salvation. As soon as she whispered those words, the nearest five nightmares immediately began scuttling towards them.

Maddock fired three times, pinning the advancing animals to the deck before the gun ran out of bolts. "You have a gun, too, Georgia. Use it!"

She aimed at the closest octopus and squeezed the trigger. The shell splattered pieces of its black shiny body all over the deck. Georgia pointed the gun at the next one and got ready to fire when Maddock placed his hand on her arm and lowered it.

"Look," he whispered. "They must be ravenous."

The remaining animals were converging on what remained of the dead octopus. Maddock took off his shoes and motioned her to do the same. They both ran silently across the deck, avoiding and jumping over the scuttling octopuses.

Maddock reached the first submersible and lifted the dome-shaped canopy. He moved to the side and motioned her to climb inside. She glanced back at the vile things before lifting herself inside. Maddock climbed in after her and closed the canopy. This machine did not belong to the resort. Georgia fastened herself into the seat beside Maddock.

"Do you know how to operate this this?"

He looked at her. "I thought you might. "

She gazed in horror at the confusing array of dials and buttons spread across the front of them. "I haven't a clue, Maddock!"

"Look, wait, don't panic. It can't be that hard." He then broke out in a wide grin and tapped a recessed panel in front of him. "I wonder." Maddock took out the handheld device and pressed it into the slot."

The Submersible's engines abruptly started and the craft began to dive.

"There we go," he replied.

Georgia pulled a deep breath into her lungs and tried to calm her racing heart. She knew that time was running out. She glanced fearfully at the water covering the canopy while watching three of those things running towards them. Maddock squeezed her hand.

"Don't worry about them. They can't hurt you now."

The machine jerked forward and raced towards an opening hatchway. "Where will this take us, Maddock?"

"Does it really matter, Georgia? As long we get away from this place before the place gets vaporised.

EPILOGUE

He swam through this lush water brimming with so many different types of new food. His old enemy and food source had perished in the blinding light along with his mate. The remaining calf had managed to escape. She had swum in the opposite direction, eager to claim her own territory.

It would be many seasons before she would be ready to receive him. Until that time, he intended to enjoy his new found freedom - and feast.

CHECK OUT OTHER GREAT DEEP SEA THRILLERS

LAMPREYS
by Alan Spencer

A secret government tactical team is sent to perform a clean sweep of a private research installation. Horrible atrocities lurk within the abandoned corridors. Mutated sea creatures with insane killing abilities are waiting to suck the blood and meat from their prey.

Unemployed college professor Conrad Garfield is forced to assist and is soon separated from the team. Alone and afraid, Conrad must use his wits to battle mutated lampreys, infected scientists and go head-to-head with the biggest monstrosity of all.

Can Conrad survive, or will the deadly monsters suck the very life from his body?

DEEP DEVOTION
by M.C. Norris

Rising from the depths, a mind-bending monster unleashes a wave of terror across the American heartland. Kate Browning, a Kansas City EMT confronts her paralyzing fear of water when she traces the source of a deadly parasitic affliction to the Gulf of Mexico. Cooperating with a marine biologist, she travels to Florida in an effort to save the life of one very special patient, but the source of the epidemic happens to be the nest of a terrifying monster, one that last rose from the depths to annihilate the lost continent of Atlantis.

Leviathan, destroyer, devoted lifemate and parent, the abomination is not going to take the extermination of its brood well.

CHECK OUT OTHER GREAT
DEEP SEA THRILLERS

PREDATOR X
by C.J Waller

When deep level oil fracking uncovers a vast subterranean sea, a crack team of cavers and scientists are sent down to investigate. Upon their arrival, they disappear without a trace. A second team, including sedimentologist Dr Megan Stoker, are ordered to seek out Alpha Team and report back their findings. But Alpha team are nowhere to be found – instead, they are faced with something unexpected in the depths. Something ancient. Something huge. Something dangerous. Predator X

DEAD BAIT
by Tim Curran

A husband hell-bent on revenge hunts a Wereshark...A Russian mail order bride with a fishy secret...Crabs with a collective consciousness...A vampire who transforms into a Candiru...Zombie piranha...Bait that will have you crawling out of your skin and more. Drawing on horror, humor with a helping of dark fantasy and a touch of deviance, these 19 contemporary stories pay homage to the monsters that lurk in the murky waters of our imaginations. If you thought it was safe to go back in the water...Think Again!

CHECK OUT OTHER GREAT DEEP SEA THRILLERS

MEGA
by Jake Bible

There is something in the deep. Something large. Something hungry. Something prehistoric.
And Team Grendel must find it, fight it, and kill it.
Kinsey Thorne, the first female US Navy SEAL candidate has hit rock bottom. Having washed out of the Navy, she turned to every drink and drug she could get her hands on. Until her father and cousins, all ex-Navy SEALS themselves, offer her a way back into the life: as part of a private, elite combat Team being put together to find and hunt down an impossible monster in the Indian Ocean. Kinsey has a second chance, but can she live through it?

THE BLACK
by Paul E Cooley

Under 30,000 feet of water, the exploration rig Leaguer has discovered an oil field larger than Saudi Arabia, with oil so sweet and pure, nations would go to war for the rights to it. But as the team starts drilling exploration well after exploration well in their race to claim the sweet crude, a deep rumbling beneath the ocean floor shakes them all to their core. Something has been living in the oil and it's about to give birth to the greatest threat humanity has ever seen.

"The Black" is a techno/horror-thriller that puts the horror and action of movies such as Leviathan and The Thing right into readers' hands. Ocean exploration will never be the same."